He moved sensually beneath her

"Your toes are curling. Join them. Let your whole body go."

"They're not!" she cried, incensed with him—and herself, finding her voice at last. Cracked, shaky, but serviceable.

"They damn well are," he murmured.

She tried to straighten her toes, and he laughed softly, triumphantly, with that cocksure male confidence that made her want to throttle him. "No!" she raged.

To her utter amazement, he pushed her away. "Oh, dear. It seems," he said lazily, his eyes burning into hers, "that I may have misinterpreted your reason for inviting me up."

SARA WOOD lives in a rambling sixteenth-century home in the medieval town of Lewes amid the Sussex hills. Her sons have claimed the cellar for bikes, making ferret cages, taxidermy and winemaking, while Sara has virtually taken over the study with her reference books, word processor and what have you. Her amiable, tolerant husband, she says, squeezes in wherever he finds room. After having tried many careers—secretary, guest house proprietor, play-group owner and primary teacher—she now finds writing romance novels gives her enormous pleasure.

Books by Sara Wood

HARLEQUIN PRESENTS

HARLEQUIN ROMANCE

SARA WOOD

Cloak of Darkness

Harlequin Books

TORONTO • NEW YORK • LONDON
AMSTERDAM • PARIS • SYDNEY • HAMBURG
STOCKHOLM • ATHENS • TOKYO • MILAN
MADRID • WARSAW • BUDAPEST • AUCKLAND

Harlequin Presents first edition July 1993
ISBN 0-373-11573-3

Original hardcover edition published in 1991
by Mills & Boon Limited

CLOAK OF DARKNESS

CHAPTER ONE

IT WASN'T a deep canal, as canals went, but that wasn't much consolation to the man who stood in it. Venetian mud was pretty disgusting. The fascinated Suzy peered into the dark night and watched as the furious man attempted to heave his legs out. He'd have a job. This particular bit of the canal system hadn't been cleaned out for years.

Oh, naughty! Her green eyes widened at the flow of profanities. Serves him right. But...*English*? With a name like his, looks like that, he ought to be Italian. Suzy shook off her surprise and started forwards, a seraphic smile on her sweet face as she moved towards her unsuspecting victim. Plans were hastily being rehashed in her fertile mind.

Carefully she tugged her drab scarf down over her face so that she'd look as ordinary and as harmless as possible. If she played her cards right, she might be able to search through his wallet.

His weight was driving him into the mud, the black gangster-coat spreading out over the dark water and dragging him down. Adding to his plight, the snow had begun to fall heavily now, the huge white flakes softening the blackness of the night and thickly covering his jet-black hair and serge-clad shoulders.

He lifted up his strong head and roared like a magnificent and furious bull into the night. 'Help me...!' He struggled to shift his legs, muttering to himself angrily, unaware of the interested bystander. 'God! How do I get out of this filth? *Mi aiuti!*' he yelled, his voice echoing around the cavernous buildings.

Poor man. She ought to put him out of his misery! 'Coming! Help is on its way!' she trilled stupidly.

He turned his head, seeing the outline of a woman approaching uncertainly along the *fondamenta*. A lamp lit her briefly, showing up her nondescript clothes, but not her features. His disappointment was clear, and Suzy could tell that he'd hoped for someone less fragile-looking to haul him out.

'English! Thank God! Go and get assistance,' he ordered, as Suzy hovered near by with mock timidity, carefully keeping her face in the shadows. 'Find a plank, a rope, and a couple of strong men. Quickly!'

'A plank, a rope, and strong men,' she repeated slowly.

She was giving herself time to observe the subtle change in him. He'd wandered about Venice over the last two days looking bored and hang-dog despite the surrounding jollity of Carnival time. Now those in-curved, hunched shoulders had straightened, his chest had expanded, and he looked as confident as any man could who stood up to his thighs in water.

'Yes! Hurry, I'm freezing!' he frowned.

'Right. Anything else, do you think?' she asked earnestly and examining him minutely. A tingle of excitement curled through her body. He *did* look different. The sagging facial muscles were taut, the straight Roman nose jutted defiantly from a newly commanding face. No one would question this man's orders—and that puzzled her. He was supposed to be a small-time crook, not a Venetian princeling.

He bit back his irritation at her slow response. 'Just get me out, please!' he said sharply, looking her straight in the eyes.

Obediently she turned away, a little disturbed by the effect of his steady gaze. There was a fierce, compelling attractiveness about him that had startled her. 'I'll try the *palazzo* over there that's being renovated. I might find a rope,' she called back over her shoulder.

Suzy had almost reached the scaffolding beside the canal when a sound stopped her dead.

From way back down the canal came the banshee scream of a police launch at full throttle. She whirled. The colour drained from her face as she realised that the man was in imminent danger. Siren blaring, headlights full on, the boat was heading straight for the helpless figure trapped in the glutinous mud.

Frantically, Suzy began to run towards the oncoming launch. 'Look out!' she shrieked to the driver. *'Attenzione!'* She waved both her arms in warning at the boat as it came screaming along the canal. She flung a look back at the trapped man.

He stood frozen with horror. Awed, she watched a spectacular fury fill his face and swell his body. Rage gave him the superhuman strength needed to fling himself forwards. With seconds left before impact, Suzy screamed and gestured wildly at the burly policeman behind the wheel, his peaked cap pulled macho-Italian style over his nose. He didn't see her, nor did he stop, the launch hurtling along crazily and filling the narrow canyon with the sound of her echoing screams, the roar of powerful engines, and the stench of diesel fumes.

And then the surge of white water which had foamed over the paving stones edging the canal receded from the horrified Suzy's feet, leaving only a slight slapping of colliding waves in the awful silence.

'Oh, dear heaven!' she whispered, nervously peering in the darkness, dreading what she might see. There was nothing. The canal was black silk again, serenely covering the filth beneath. And now, maybe a body.

Suzy drew in a ragged breath, too shocked to take in the full implications. This was her fault. Dear God! She could have saved him if she'd gone to his rescue some seconds earlier. Her hand lifted to her mouth to stifle a groan of bitter regret and despair. Back-street canals weren't deep; his plight had been vaguely funny, not alarming.

High jinks or accidents, more people fell into canals at Carnival time than during the whole year. It was pure luck that she'd been around. She'd just decided to stop following him for the night, since he was on his way home. And now... Anxiously Suzy searched the water, her heart pounding violently.

To her utter relief, there was a surge of silver by the high-arched bridge spanning the canal ahead. From the blackness there rose a pale, ghostly face.

Her eyes closed in brief and fervent thanks. Small-time gangster he might be, but no one deserved to be sliced up by the hull of a boat. Feeling suddenly sick, Suzy stumbled along the stone-flagged walkway. The dark head shook itself like a dog and swivelled two glowing black eyes in her direction.

'Get me *out* of here!' the man spluttered, beside himself with fury, white teeth snarling in his dark, contorted face.

Trembling all over, she crouched down on the edge of the *fondamenta*, her face still in deep shadow. 'Thank heavens you're alive!' she breathed jerkily, staring at him wide-eyed across the dividing water.

'Let's skip the service of thanksgiving,' he said curtly. 'Action first, prayers later.'

'You're not hurt?' She let out her breath in a rush of air and felt the tension going from her body, leaving it weak.

'No. Winded.' He glared into the darkness ahead where the police boat had disappeared, and Suzy could see from his clenched jaw and the sinews in his neck that he was violently cursing the driver under his breath and struggling to control his temper in her presence.

That puzzled her. A considerate crook? 'You're very lucky,' she cried with some passion. 'I thought you were dead!'

'So did I. So did we all,' he said harshly. 'Do you mind if we stop having these long conversations? I'm sinking into this damn mud. Don't bother to go for help, there isn't time. Get that rope, anything.'

'Of course.' Apologetically, Suzy jumped up and hurried back to the scaffolded palace.

Mercifully he had no idea that she'd been following him. But she'd blown her cover now. So she'd help him and hope to befriend him. Pleased, Suzy scrambled over a pile of rotting timber. The Contessa had instructed her to watch where he went, who he talked to, and what he did. The man was apparently blackmailing the Contessa, and it was Suzy's job to discover anything that could be used as a counter-threat against him. So far, she'd drawn a blank.

She grinned, enjoying the excitement of it all now that the danger had passed, and feeling the intoxication of risk-taking bubbling inside her.

'Haven't you found anything yet?' he asked irritably.

'No rope,' she answered, clambering around the cement-mixer.

There was a ghastly squelching sound and she turned to see that he was trying in vain to lift his feet from the deep silt. He didn't give up. His face set in determined lines as he remorselessly willed his powerful body to obey him.

'See if the builders have left a ladder,' he ordered.

'I've found a plank,' she called, heaving it out of the pile of builders' debris. She dragged it to the edge of the canal and leaned out over the water as far as she dared, pushing the plank in his direction. Too vigorously, it appeared.

'Ooof!' He'd lunged forwards and grabbed at it, but it had kept coming. The plank had crushed the air from his lungs, yet he hung on, coughing violently. His baleful dark eyes flashed to her face, narrowing to study it intently. A look of wariness came into his expression and she wondered with a spurt of alarm whether he *had* seen her tailing him and had recognised her face now it was only a few feet away.

'Whoops!' she said with a stupid laugh. She saw his eyes on a lock of her long, rather identifiable brown hair, and hastily tucked it beneath her scarf. 'My mistake! I'm not too good at this kind of thing. Catch hold,' she urged merrily. 'We'll have you out in two ticks. The temperature of that water must be freezing.' She beamed in sympathy.

'Nice touch,' he gritted with a sour expression. 'The Slug-Him-and-Smile technique. Have another try. Carefully. This time slide it down *near* me, not *at* me.' He paused while the cough racked his body harshly again. 'Then—unless you have other plans—I can haul myself out,' he finished sarcastically.

There had definitely been a change in his attitude, she thought warily. He was like an animal at bay, alert and watchful, ready to defend himself at all cost. Suzy increased her vapid innocence to allay his suspicions.

'It's a very heavy plank,' she pouted. 'I'm doing my best.' Ungrateful swine! She shoved the plank deep into the mud and balanced the other end on the edge of the walkway beside the canal. 'Come on, you can make it,' she encouraged.

With a shower of water, he raised his arms and a pair of massive hands grabbed the plank. He took a deep breath and dragged himself up the slope, sheer brute strength and grit causing his legs and feet to be drawn from the imprisoning mud with an unpleasant, squashy, sucking sound.

Suzy's eyes narrowed. He must be as brawny as a blacksmith to do that. A real toughie. She wondered about his background. Some dockside tenement, where Rambo ruled OK? It was another observation for her notebook. She'd have a lot to tell the Contessa tomorrow morning.

His hand reached for hers and she grasped it, finding her fist being slowly compressed by an iron vice as he drew himself towards her. Suzy gasped. She kept herself fit, she had developed strength in her hands to climb drainpipes if necessary, she had trained with some impressively muscle-bound men, but she'd never encountered anyone with a grip like his. He could crush ribs with his fingers. No wonder the Contessa had told her to be careful. And his glare was enough to strip paint alone.

Wonderful! She felt adrenalin sear through her veins at the thought of a worthy adversary at last. This assignment promised to be rather exciting. Her eyes glowed with enthusiasm.

'Enjoying this?' he growled.

His hand tightened on hers and she winced, furious with herself for showing what she was thinking.

'Who, me? Of course not! It's just that your hand is bringing tears to my eyes, that's all. You're so *strong*! Almost there,' she said in a strained voice, wondering if her knuckles were mashed yet.

He grunted, single-mindedly intent on reaching the edge. 'Pull, damn you!' he muttered. Stubbornly she stopped trying, longing to let him slide back into the water. His hostile eyes blistered her with one contemptuous glance, and his chin jutted out aggressively. 'When I get out of here——' he continued, in a threatening tone.

'Yes,' she interrupted sweetly, thinking of how she'd twist him around her little finger. 'Won't it be nice?'

She grabbed his coat-collar with her free hand and suddenly tugged with all her might. Unfortunately, his body shot forwards, his chin shooting up and dropping again to catch the top of the plank with a resounding thud. To her alarm, the thick-lashed lids slowly closed and he rolled in a black, sodden and stinking heap at her feet.

What had she done? she thought in alarm. Suzy's hesitant finger tested the pulse at his neck. It still beat strongly, much to her relief. Crouching down, she slipped her hand under his heavy coat, sliding her palm over the swelling curve of his big chest. His heart thudded like a stallion's, warm and even beneath her hand. Suzy felt a faint blush spread over her face. She was unaccustomed to raiding men's bodies; it seemed such an intimate thing to do.

'Drat!' she muttered, withdrawing her hand and wondering what to do with him. He'd be no good to her like this. And yet... She eyed the huddled figure thoughtfully. Every cloud had a silver lining, for wasn't he now helpless and at her mercy? Fate had delivered him. She couldn't have asked for a better scenario.

He was the Contessa's enemy. He intended to harm Flavia Moroschini—a tragic figure, confined for the rest of her life to a wheelchair. Suzy's eyes hardened. This man was a villain and deserved no pity, so she needn't pussy-foot around. Warily, watching the glistening black lashes for any sign of movement, she gingerly, hesitantly extracted his wallet and pocketed it.

Close to him for the first time, she saw that his face had become ashen, his lips the colour of stone. Her eyes roamed over his high forehead, which was softened by the heavy, wayward waves that up to now had been ruthlessly restrained. His cheekbones formed two perfectly carved planes above the hollow of his cheeks, and the sculptor Donatello would have been proud to have created the pure, clean jawline. As for the expressive mouth, smiled Suzy, it was more Italian than English. The softly curving lips parted and let out a groan.

'Wake up!' she said urgently.

He sank heavily into unconsciousness again, and Suzy sighed. Common criminal or not, she had to do something with him. Somehow she had to get him back on his feet, cleaned up, repaired and raring to go, without involving the ambulance service or the police. Be discreet, the Contessa had said. No scandal. Perhaps...

'Oh, if you only knew the indignity I'm going to inflict on you,' she whispered cheerfully to the lifeless man. Her hand touched the firm skin over his prominent cheekbones in an affectionate gesture. He was giving her the time of her life. This was what she'd always wanted to do—pit her wits against a real criminal.

Humming to herself, she left him for a moment to collect one of the small-wheeled trolleys used by the builders, the only kind of wheeled traffic allowed in Venice. Then, bracing herself and using her weight training to good advantage, she clasped her arms around his chest and began to lift. It was amazing the rats she'd picked up, she thought in wry amusement.

The rat stiffened in her arms. His heavy black brows angled to meet over his nose. 'What...?'

Suzy looked down at his dazed, half-closed eyes, 'Just a little ride,' she coaxed.

'No!' Shaken as he was, he managed to stand, leaning heavily on her. 'I've heard that line in gangster movies. God, my head!' In an appealing gesture, his hand swept over his forehead, releasing diamond droplets of water on to her upturned face. He staggered, and the trolley rolled back into the canal before she could grab it.

She sighed regretfully. It would have been funny. Now she'd have a tough time getting him back. Resigning herself to the struggle, she tucked her shoulder beneath his arm. 'Come on. We'll make it together.'

'Thanks,' he said in a barely audible voice.

Suzy wilted beneath his weight, but she kept doggedly on, guiding his footsteps, steering him over the thick snow through the narrow, deserted alleys to her flat.

She had Venice to herself. It was too late for Carnival revellers, too early for the barges and trolleys bringing food and goods from the four corners of the earth. Beneath her feet, the snow was fresh and virginal. The city lay hushed and asleep. The funeral-black gondolas, bobbing at their moorings, were now dredged with snow and bridal white and, despite her exhaustion, Suzy's heart swelled with a quiet joy that she was there.

For four years now she'd lived in the city and had never tired of it. *He'd* tired her that day, though, wretched man—wandering aimlessly through Venice as if he didn't have a clue what he was doing, slipping into bars for pastries and hot coffee while she had shivered outside, resenting his smug, satisfied face as he had sat in the warmth indoors.

Her feet were killing her, her calf muscles ached, she'd been looking forward to a bath and bed. Now he'd flung himself into the canal, she was having to mother him, too. But the tempo and the direction of her assignment had taken such a different turn that it had revitalised her and filled her with exhilaration.

'Not far,' she said with relief as they crossed the tiny bridge over a back-street canal.

He had been in a mindless daze, it seemed, because he stumbled and groaned deeply, clutching his chest. 'Not far where? Oh, hell. Stop a moment!' he jerked out hoarsely.

She leant him up against a dark brick wall, where he stared at her with bleary eyes. His longish hair was plastered to his forehead like a series of black commas and there was a slight swelling on his jaw. She'd patch him up as good as new and earn herself Brownie points into the bargain.

'You'll be safe and warm soon,' she said in a syrupy voice. 'It's just around the corner.' Suzy skilfully draped his arm around her shoulder and took the brunt of his weight again for a few steps. 'Well done! Here we are.' She came to a halt outside a tiny medieval building in a narrow street. He was sagging alarmingly in her arms, and she could barely keep him upright. 'Upsadaisy! Can you manage a few stairs?' she enquired sweetly.

'Stairs? What... where are we?' he mumbled incoherently. He touched his jaw and winced, letting her draw him upright. He staggered again and she held him firmly, her back arching with the effort.

If he stayed confused much longer, she thought in concern, she'd have to get Guido to give him the once-over. 'Come along,' she said encouragingly, like a mother to a slow-witted child, and propping him against the wall. He began to slide and she leaned hard against him, resigning herself to the fact that her clothes were being ruined by mud and water. Placing her hand firmly under his armpit and wedging her body against his, she unlocked the door. 'Well, this is it!'

He stood rock solid. His arms clamped around her, crushing her to his hard body in a semblance of an embrace. Suzy was aware of the stolen wallet in her pocket pressing into his wet thigh, and tried to heave him away, but he stumbled a little, and she guiltily felt the shape of the wallet burn its imprint between them.

'Oh...' His heavy-lidded eyes seemed to melt into hers. 'Goodnight, darling,' he mumbled.

Suzy stiffened as he swung automatically into what was obviously his normal routine when plastered against a woman beside a doorway. Scornfully she registered the kind of females he must take out. Bar-room pick-ups. It figured. She glared up at him and saw that his eyes looked drugged and warm, his mouth so beautifully curving and sensual that if she hadn't known who he was—and what he was—she would gladly have surrendered her lips to his. The discovery shocked her.

'This is not goodnight——' she began firmly, struggling in his iron embrace.

'No? There's more?' he mumbled, his mouth soft. 'Bad girl,' he slurred happily, and clumsily aimed for her lips.

She twisted her head away to avoid his bumbling, inept attempt at a kiss, and his mouth landed on the wool scarf, his lips so hot that they burned warm and moist into her ear. Distracted, it was a moment before she discovered that his hands were roughly squeezing her buttocks—and then, to her outrage, sliding up beneath her coat and groping for her breasts.

He had the sexual technique of a bull elephant. Incensed, Suzy used her arms as a lever against his coarsely tweaking hands, thrusting them up and out, then twisting away to free herself. With enormous satisfaction, she stamped hard on his foot. Making no effort to retaliate, he rocked slightly and blinked at her stupidly with innocent, hurt eyes, and she realised he was still half stunned and not responsible for his actions.

'Wake *up*!' she snapped in a sharp, cracking command.

His hands dropped to her hips, rotating as if they were on automatic pilot. Contempt for his rough-and-ready method of courting a woman made her mouth turn down sourly. Weren't there any decent men in this world, to match up to the decent women?

'I'm waking,' he husked. 'Who are you? Do I know you?' he asked, baffled.

Suzy stopped breathing for a moment in trepidation, as his hands roamed with rough enthusiasm almost as if he was frisking her. Without success, she reached down and tried to pull them away. Surely he'd notice the wallet in her pocket? But he seemed to be occupied in working out what was going on, shaking his head in a perplexed way. Fortunately he was totally disorientated.

'No, I'm just a Good Samaritan,' she said, grim-faced and wriggling from his arms at last. 'That's enough! In!' She pushed him, crossly.

He lurched into the unlit hall and recovered a little, peering into the gloom, and she knew immediately by the tensing of his body that his sixth sense was working and had been alerted to potential danger. She'd have to go carefully.

'I can't see a damn thing. Where's the light?' he complained in a laboured voice.

'There isn't one. We'll have to go up in the dark.'

His big body went rigid and she couldn't budge him. 'Go where?' he demanded truculently, his eyes glinting in the gloom. 'What's going on?'

Suzy patted his chest reassuringly. Whatever it did for him, the action wasn't very reassuring to her. His body felt hard and poised for action. Her instincts had been right; he'd recovered faster than his face and manner suggested, and she wondered just how confused he really was.

'I'm helping you. This is the way up to my flat. You're in no fit state to go home alone, so I'm going to look after you till you recover. You fell in the canal——'

'Like hell, I did! I'm perfectly aware I was pushed,' he growled.

She stiffened, her mind whirling, turning over the idea, and she wished she could see his face clearly. The claim was far-fetched, but possible. She'd witnessed the accident. That furtive figure dressed in the cape and carnival mask *could* have deliberately pushed him. If so, why? A joke? Or was he blackmailing someone else, as well as the Contessa? Her mouth curved down in disdain. He was the lowest of the low.

'Whatever happened to you, you need a bit of attention,' she said crisply. 'You're shivering. Come on, it's only me and my flat. I can hardly hurt a big, strong man like you, can I?' she cooed, remembering she was supposed to encourage him.

Her eyes were getting used to the dark and she realised that he was scowling at her. He was coming to his senses and getting nastier by the minute. 'Don't patronise me,' came his cold voice, slicing the darkness. 'I'm weakened physically, not mentally. You're as tough as nails and as sturdy as an ox. I've felt your muscles and I know how toned your body is. You could probably fell most men with a blow of your fist.'

Suzy quickly closed her mouth, which had dropped open in astonishment. 'A girl has to work out nowadays,' she said archly, fluttering her lashes at him.

'Hmm. Maybe you've got someone up there, waiting to jump me?'

'Good grief, this is Venice, not the Bronx! You've got a really suspicious mind,' she said placidly. 'I'm doing my good turn for the day. I'm cold too, you know. Do come up.'

'What for, the last rites?' he asked sarcastically. 'Are you the back-up team?'

'Oh, *please*!' she wailed, losing her patience with him. 'Just look at you, dripping slime and sludge on to the floor! It'll take me ages to clear this up. I suppose you could walk back to wherever you're staying, but you'd risk double pneumonia in this weather. And no water taxi would take you in that state.'

'Why should I trust you?' he asked sourly. 'God knows what plans you have for me.'

'Plans? What could I do to a great big hunk of a man like you?' she asked, widening her eyes, hoping he could see her innocence. 'Oh, come on!' she coaxed. 'Haven't you ever heard of sheer human kindness before?'

'No.'

'Oh, lord. Come up,' she said, with genuine sympathy, sensing a wealth of meaning in that bleak monosyllable. She quailed at the pain in his dark eyes. It looked as if he had suffered life, blow by blow, from the moment he had been born. A missionary zeal flowed through her, a sympathy far beyond any she *ought* to feel for this bad-tempered, chauvinistic gangster.

'Why should you help me?' he asked suspiciously.

'Why shouldn't I?' Suzy's gentle voice warmed the air between them. Who knew what an awful upbringing he'd had? Maybe if she befriended him, she could persuade him to leave the Contessa alone. Impulsively she held out her hand and, when he made no move to respond, she took his ice-cold fingers in hers. 'Dry clothes, a hot shower, a meal. How's that sound?'

'Paradise,' he admitted grudgingly, 'though I'm sure there's a snake in this Eden somewhere, to spoil it.' He drew in a shuddery breath. 'God, I'm cold! OK. But no funny business, or as sure as hell you'll regret it.'

'Oh, your virtue is safe with me,' she said chirpily, going on ahead.

He grunted. 'It's not my virtue I'm worried about.'

Suzy's confidence in handling the situation increased when she realised that he was finding the almost vertical stairs difficult to manage. He'd be incapable of raising the energy to harm her. After all, he was carrying an extra ton weight in water and mud. He would be grateful. He'd be in her debt. They'd have a cosy chat over the cocoa. She beamed, planning her questions, dying to know all about him.

Busy with her thoughts, she totally forgot to warn him about the worn step at the top, where the centuries-old stone had broken away. In the dark he missed his footing, slid down a few steps and cracked his shin, letting out an almighty expletive.

'Let go my damn hair!' he growled.

'I had to grab something,' she defended huffily, releasing the handful of thick, wet waves. 'It was all I could find in the dark.' She helped him up, finding her face inches from his. A cold, tingling sensation ran over her skin as his icy breath hit her lips in the darkness.

'If I thought for one cotton-pickin' moment that you did that on purpose...' His savage, pained whisper trailed away meaningfully.

Suzy felt a chill run down her spine. 'Why would I want to do that?' she said, pouting.

'You tell me,' he snarled.

The helpless victim had disappeared, and so had the stunned groper, leaving the real villain—mean, moody and menacing. So she would take the wind out of his sails and refuse to be menaced. Besides, she had to convince him she was an innocent bystander with no *reason* to find him threatening, or she'd be wallowing in trouble. The Contessa had said he had an inflated ego, a sense of his own importance. She hid a smile. She'd work on his vanity, his Achilles' heel.

'I don't know how you can think that of me,' she protested, sounding hurt. From somewhere in her boots, she dragged out a husky, seductive voice. 'I wouldn't want your body... spoiled. It's too *hunky* for that,' she said suggestively, her hand reaching out and touching his face in awe. 'I'd forgotten about the step. You put it clean out of my mind. I have bruises from it too.' She gave a little laugh. 'We'll have to compare legs in a minute,' she giggled, letting her hand rest on his warm neck in an affectionate gesture. And a little stroke of his hair... She smirked as he growled in his throat. 'You can put witch-hazel on my bruise, I'll put some on yours,' she promised.

'Well I'll be——!' he muttered. 'You do know how to coax a man, don't you?'

He caught her fingers in his teeth and nuzzled them. She resisted her desire to snatch them away, and made little noises in her throat, too. It seemed to be the thing to do. The stairway suddenly seemed hot and confining. Suzy wanted to find some space for herself. So she patted his face and caught hold of his big hand, leading him on and feeling strangely uncomfortable about what she was doing.

But she had no option. She couldn't abandon him. She couldn't arouse his suspicions. That left deceit. And a nasty taste in her mouth. Plus the danger of it... Her eyes sparkled. Her whole body was tingling with expectation.

'We're here,' she panted, coming to the top of the fourth flight, waiting for him to toil up. Odd that he wasn't breathing heavily, she thought. Her mind sharpened up a few more notches. He was wet, not weak. She ought to keep on her toes and not underestimate him.

When she switched on the hall light, however, the glaring light bulb told a different story. It was apparent that he'd been manfully fighting his discomfort. He looked absolutely terrible—bedraggled and exhausted, his clothes covered in mud, his feet in a large, evil-looking puddle, his face pale and drawn. She drew back a little, shaken by the intensely male sexuality that was thickening the air. Even in this state, he was dominant, threatening, dangerous. He swayed and then shivered.

'My goodness, you could do with a complete overhaul,' she said, sternly hiding her alarm. 'Here's the bathroom. In there, quick, before you ruin my rug. Take your things off and dump them in the bath.' She felt more secure, being bossy. Men loathed bossy women.

His broad shoulders slumped wearily against the wall. He curled his fingers up slowly to fumble with the buttons of his coat. A deep scowl appeared on his forehead. Grimly determined, he kept trying. A shudder of cold rippled through him, and he held his hands in front of his sodden coat, staring at them in exasperation, to the sound of the slow drip, drip of water and splatter of mud.

'I can't,' he muttered, frowning harder as his teeth chattered violently. 'They won't damn well obey me!'

'Let me.'

He seemed perplexed, as if he was totally surprised at his uncharacteristic physical weakness. Suzy moved his icy hands aside gently and undid the heavy black coat, stretching up on tiptoe to slide it from his shoulders. No label—and too wet to estimate its quality. It fell to the floor with a watery squelch. Then she removed his denim jacket in the same way.

It gave her no clues, allowing her no information about his lifestyle. It had good stitching, but wasn't special and the label had been removed, too. She frowned. The shirt looked as if it had been made in Hong Kong and could have cost anything. The fit was perfect, but that might be due to his perfect body.

However, Suzy knew that generally crooks dressed to impress, wearing designer-label clothes and flashing their money around when they had any. He was living as cheaply as he could in Venice, and she'd judged him to be a low-ranking criminal. She could cope with riff-raff. Her hands chafed his briskly and, as they did so, she casually pushed up his soggy cuff. Chain-store watch, plastic strap. One signet ring with an eagle on it. Unmarried.

'Can you do your own jeans?' she asked hopefully. Undressing men was something she ought to charge danger-money for.

He made a supreme effort, and she felt a sudden, surprising flicker of admiration for him, seeing a grit and a determination that matched hers. Unfortunately his hands were numb and unresponsive. Placing her hand on his chest, she felt how cold he was, and realised that his breathing was becoming very shallow. The shock was beginning to set in. She must get him warm.

'This is infuriating! I *can't*!' he gritted through his waywardly juddering teeth, furious in his frustration and helplessness.

Suzy's face softened. So he was proud, too, not used to being dependent on people. Just like her, she thought, and it made a kind of fragile bond between them. 'I'll do it,' she said gently. 'Come on. We must get something warm into you.'

'A big, beautiful bottle of brandy?' he shivered.

'Why not?' Her fingers began to undo the belt-buckle, and she felt him draw back with a slight stiffness, tensing his exhausted body. 'Relax,' she said softly, trying to placate his male dignity. 'Pretend I'm your mother.'

He winced. 'I would if I knew what a mother was like,' he said flatly.

'You must have had a mother,' she said with a faint frown, delicately drawing down his zip and moving discreetly behind him, her face turning pink with embarrassment.

'In passing. My birth, her death,' he said curtly.

Suzy's expression softened with genuine warmth. 'Poor you,' she commented quietly. 'Make it an auntie, then.'

He glowered round at her. 'Are you trying to be funny?' he snarled.

'Not consciously,' she replied in surprise.

Was it something she'd said? He looked very annoyed. After a brief pause while she drew back the waistband of his jeans and surreptitiously investigated the label of his black boxer-shorts—product of Hong Kong again and impossible to price—she let the jeans fall soggily to his ankles, to reveal a pair of strong, masculine legs. Tanned legs, very touchable, with a series of white scars on one thigh. Suzy shifted uncomfortably, finding the situation a little too intimate. She forced herself to concentrate on her job, hoping to begin an exchange of information.

'Sorry if I've hit a nerve,' she said, deciding to chatter. 'But you're in good company. I have a similar background to you, by the sound of it. My mother abandoned me. She must have been in an awful state to do that, don't you think?' she offered in a conversational tone. She spoke in an attempt to dissipate the tense atmosphere. She tossed his jeans into the bath. 'I was brought up in a children's home. One big, happy family—though a bit of peace and quiet would——' Her voice faltered at his sour expression, and she changed tack. 'At least you were luckier than me. You had a father,' she pointed out.

'No. I didn't,' he snapped, and shivered again.

'Oh. Did he die, too?' she asked sadly.

'As good as,' he muttered.

Suzy sensed his resentment towards his absentee father. Family life had given him a miss. It explained a lot. She had another go. 'Aren't you brown?' she smiled, lathering on the admiration. 'No wonder you're feeling the cold. I suppose you've just come back from holiday. Somewhere nice?'

'Cut out the chat,' he growled. 'I'm not in the mood.'

She resisted the urge to growl back. Somehow she had to get him all soft and malleable. He sat wearily on the bathroom stool. Bending down, she submissively untied his laces and eased off his trainers, then peeled off his socks, rubbing his bare feet between her hands to warm them.

She reached up to ease off his tie and became very conscious of the nearness of his mobile mouth. Mechanically she undid his shirt buttons. The big chest felt as hard as iron to the sensitive tips of her fingers. He swayed on the chair and her palms flattened to hold him steady, lingering on the smooth skin, a small tremor going through her while she waited for him to right himself and stop gripping her shoulders so tightly as if he was testing the strength of her muscles. He was looking at her with a bleak expression.

Her eyes warmed. 'I'll look after you. You'll be OK,' she said quietly.

'Write me a guarantee,' he muttered.

Suzy smiled and concentrated on sliding off his shirt. Glorious torso. Hardly any hair—she loathed hairy chests. This one was smooth and shapely. She showed him into her bed-sit, found him a blanket, and motioned for him to sit by the electric fire. He huddled into the blanket, sitting hunched on the edge of a chair, his face surly. And she could see his brain working.

'I'll make you a hot drink, first,' she said with a sickly smile.

His eyes swivelled to hers, watchful, menacing. She plastered an even brighter smile on her face, trying to look vaguely idiotic, and yet suspicion kept coming at her in lethal waves. To hide her unease, she turned to the little stove in the corner of the room and clattered about fussily with the kettle, still wearing her coat and scarf. They seemed to protect her somehow.

If he suspected her—that she'd been shadowing him and reporting his every move... She dropped the filter papers. He came over and picked them up before she had time to bend, his big body rising up deliberately close to hers, pure male sexuality intimidating her. She laid her hand on a kitchen knife, ready.

CHAPTER TWO

'NERVOUS about something?' the man asked silkily, his eyes glittering. The light behind him, which bathed her in a pool of amber, haloed his hair with gold, and a gilded line curved around his powerful neck and shoulders, painting the muscular biceps. A faint steam rose from his body so that he looked like a black-haired devil ascending from hell.

Suzy lifted her gaze from his daunting pectoral muscles. This situation was probably nothing new to him, but it was to her, and she was finding it surprisingly difficult to cope.

'Yes, of course! You see, I'm not used to having a man in my room,' she simpered coyly, deciding to bluff it out. It was true that she was nervous. A half-naked, lawless crook, hewn from the living rock, would make any woman quiver. And her instincts told her that there was a slumbering intent about him which spelled danger.

Her hand fluttered to her breast and his eyes went there like a homing-pigeon. His mouth curled with sensual contempt as if he was used to women trembling when he put on the passion. To dispel her feeling of agitation, Suzy whisked off the loathsome scarf. Her waist-length brown hair flowed out down her back in a cascade of tiny, rippling waves. Stupid, stupid! she groaned to herself, at his deep, appreciative inhalation.

'Very effective,' he mocked softly. 'With timing like that, you don't have to worry about any lack of experience. Your sense of the theatrical is impressive. So now I'm almost naked and you've revealed your crowning

glory. What's next?' His dark eyes glittered as she kicked
her shoes off sullenly. 'Strippers usually leave those on,'
he advised in a well-meaning tone. 'They'd go for the
coat next.'

She'd go for the jugular, if he didn't stop making
suggestive remarks, she thought angrily. Gritting her
teeth, she turned the kettle with apparent absent-
mindedness so that the steam shot up in his face and he
took a step back, his mouth tightening and losing its
carnality. She held down her smile of satisfaction and
ignored his gibe, turning innocent eyes on him.

'Strippers?' she gurgled, giving him a little push,
cleverly moving him further back. 'You are a scream!'
She indicated her dull brown coat. 'Anyone less like a
stripper...' Leaving the sentence hanging scornfully in
mid-air, she smiled prettily. 'Were you having a lark out
there, on the canal? Was it a friend of yours who pushed
you in?' she asked with just the right amount of
amusement, as if it were all a great joke.

His dark eyes surveyed her thoughtfully for a moment.
'Not a friend. A bungling fool who made a terrible
mistake,' he said softly. 'When I catch up with him, I'll
break his neck.'

He would, too, she thought nervously. 'Do you want
to ring the police now?' she asked brightly, knowing full
well he wouldn't want that. Crooks kept a low profile.
'You must report the driver of the police launch,' she
said earnestly. 'He could have killed you. Odd he didn't
see you, wasn't it, when those headlights were so bright?'

His mouth thinned. 'Very odd. I'll ring later. The
driver must be insane,' he said savagely. 'When I find
out who it was,' he continued in a low growl, his malevolent eyes fixed on her, 'I'll ruin his sex-life for ever.'

'My, you're going to be busy!' Suzy shivered inside,
some of her self-confidence evaporating. Judging by his
meaningful look, it seemed that he was accusing her of

being involved. Her eyes opened in alarm. He couldn't think that she…? She licked dry lips and spooned coffee into the cone of filter paper, conscious of his brooding eyes watching every movement she made. 'I tried to stop him,' she husked. 'I did all I could.' She swallowed, pinned like a wriggling insect by his relentless eyes. 'I yelled out to you——'

'I couldn't move,' he said softly. 'You must have known that. How long had you been there, watching me struggle?'

'Me? I'd just arrived——'

'How fortunate.'

'You're darn right it was!' she snapped huffily, fed up with his insinuations. 'You'd be dead if it wasn't for me.'

He gave her a scathing, disbelieving look, and went to sit by the fire again. 'Hurry up with that coffee. I'll be dead from pneumonia in a moment.'

'I'm doing my best,' she said crossly. 'And you can mind your manners. I don't have to do this.'

'Why are you, then?' he shot back.

'I'm writing a thesis on drowning rats,' she snapped. There was a silence. She could have kicked herself, but the remark had been long coming. It rather ruined her simpering girly act, though. She wasn't much good at deception, she thought gloomily.

'Drowned many rats lately?' he drawled, warming his hands.

'One too few.'

There was the suspicion of a smile creaking up the corner of his lips. 'You certainly failed tonight. Is that why you're annoyed?' he murmured.

'I'm annoyed because I did you a favour and you're being plain bad-tempered.'

'So would you be, in my position,' he said quietly.

Suzy heaved a huge sigh. 'Yes,' she conceded, nodding. 'I'd be absolutely blazing mad. Don't take it out on me, though. I'm tired after a hard day——'

'Oh. Been on your feet a long time?'

A chill settled on her spine. 'Ages. I am doing my best to make you comfortable.' Her bland smile was received with a cynically raised eyebrow.

'Don't overdo the charm,' he said coldly. 'From where I'm sitting, it's looking a little synthetic at the edges. The honeyed words have become . . . tacky.'

'I don't know what you mean.'

Turning back to the stove, Suzy tried to shake off the ominous tension that was mounting in the room. He was deeply suspicious and alert, adrenalin tangibly pumping through his body. Unbearably hot, she slid off her coat and threw it on to a chair, glad that her dress was a plain one. She looked down at her body, trying to see what he would see.

Her lips parted in faint dismay. The green jersey was clinging to her warm body as it never had before, shaping her full breasts and small waist, emphasising her womanly hips. Suzy felt more and more edgy. She'd dealt with small-time criminals, but none like this one. There had been something about the way he'd looked at her that was more than purely sensual or calculating . . . She paused to search for the word. Inhuman. Goose-pimples ran up her arms at the thought of the revenge he'd take on people who double-crossed him or got in his way.

The infuriating thing was that he suspected her of something she hadn't done. If she was to protect the helpless Contessa from him, she had to improve her performance. Everything depended on her. She practised a smile, polished it and perfected it before turning.

'Your coffee's ready,' she said cheerfully, pouring it into a mug and handing it to him.

His hands closed around it and he gave a relentless stare in response to her artificially bright face. 'Bit mean on the brandy,' he frowned, after taking a tentative sip.

Suzy's mouth compressed. Being nice to him wasn't easy. 'Brandy later. Finish it up, have a hot shower, and then you can get smashed out of your mind, if that's what you want. Feeling warmer?'

'Marginally.' He cradled the mug and his big frame shook with a deep shiver which made him wince. 'My ribs hurt, my shins hurt, my jaw aches and my head feels like it's going round on a race-track, all on its own. Other than that, life's never been sweeter.' His aristocratic nostrils flared. 'I can't *wait* to find out what tomorrow will bring, in this god-forsaken city. It's given me a welcome I'll never forget. Maybe a brick will drop off the *campanile* and brain me, or the pigeons in the *piazza* will peck me to death.'

Suzy laughed delightedly. 'Oh, dear! You don't like Venice, then,' she observed with malicious pleasure. Perhaps he'd leave if he hated it enough.

'I don't like Venetians,' he scowled. He followed her to the small shower cabinet in the alcove behind the curtains, and she knew he was deliberately crowding her while she fiddled with the controls. 'One tries to drown me, one to run me down. I haven't worked out your role in it all yet.'

'Me? I'm the one who saved your life,' she reminded him sweetly. 'It occurred to me that *someone* ought to haul you out of the canal before the launch got you on its way back.' That flippant remark had been a mistake. Suzy quailed at the malevolent glitter which had leapt into his eyes. 'Sorry,' she apologised quickly. 'Joke. Not very funny, under the circumstances. Stupid of me.'

'It was. Very.' He handed her the blanket. 'I would have thought,' he said coldly, 'that the launch was a teensy bit over the top, wasn't it? The poisonous filth from that water is probably enough to give me a slow and painful death. Much more satisfying for all concerned than a quick, merciful release.'

Suzy gave a nervous laugh. Her mind whirled. He seemed convinced that the whole thing had been engineered. Revenge in Italy was violent and swift, but she could hardly believe that one of this man's victims would organise such an elaborate accident.

'You do have a vivid imagination!' she smiled. 'You just had two accidents, that's all. Coincidences. But you're right. I think you should have some injections in the morning. I could recommend a doctor,' she said helpfully, thinking of Guido. Now *that* would be an interesting meeting. 'He's awfully good——'

'I'm sure he is,' said the man in a tired voice. 'But I'd rather risk the germs. Just what were you doing, out so late?' he suddenly shot at her.

She blinked. 'What was I doing?' she repeated, trying to think at the same time. 'Oh. Washing up,' she said, seeing his eyes narrowing and kicking herself for the second's hesitation. 'I'm a domestic,' she said blithely, using her standard pretence for visiting palaces. It stopped the staff and neighbours from gossiping and knowing her true purpose. No one wanted to broadcast the fact that they were employing a private detective. 'I cook,' she answered truthfully, 'serve meals and wash up. It's ever so interesting.'

He grimaced at the silly way she spoke, and heaved a deep sigh, expanding his chest so that there seemed to be a vast acreage of hilly torso. Wall-to-wall flesh. Suzy's eyes widened a little and lingered.

'There's a viewing fee,' he drawled.

'Cash in while you can,' she said dead-pan. 'That bruise on your ribs is spectacular enough to win a prize. Hurry up and shower and I'll make you as good as new afterwards.'

'Doctors and nurses,' he murmured. 'What fun.'

Suzy's mouth fell open in surprise, but he'd stepped into the shower and she was left staring at the opaque curtain swinging an inch from her nose. And then the general shape of his naked body. She blinked, quickly turned, and went to find something to eat.

Wearily she pushed herself to keep going. Remaining sharp-witted had been exhausting, and her spirits were beginning to wilt. On top of a hard day, it was proving to be too much. Oh, for bed! And someone to deliver a pizza...

Steam began to fill the apartment. But there were no sounds of vigorous soaping going on, only a slow, laborious splashing, as if he couldn't manage anything more energetic. She hoped he was all right. The shower was switched off, she heard the curtain being drawn aside and the soft sound of a towel being wrapped around a wet body. She chopped peppers with great care. It had been a long time since she was alone in a bedroom with a man, and she wasn't too sure about this one.

The last occasion had been five years ago. Mario. Her eyes grew bleak and her fingers paused at the twinge of hurt which ran through her body. To be honest, she'd never really been alone with him, even though he'd been her husband. What a hell it had been! The whole of his family had slept on the other side of the cardboard-thin walls of their bedroom, and this had relegated their lovemaking to furtive movements. She sighed ruefully. It hadn't been too bright of her to get married to a chauvinist who had no money and lived in a Naples slum.

She bit her lip hard and crushed a clove of garlic, as if it had offended her deeply.

Suddenly her preoccupation with her own thoughts was driven away by the total silence in the room. Turning, she saw that the man was leaning weakly against the wall with his eyes closed, still dripping wet from his shower.

His lashes were black and wet on his cheeks, glistening drops of water raining down from the heavy locks of hair on his forehead.

Vulnerable and unguarded, his face looked quite different. His brows were drawn together in a faint frown, his lips parted and slightly sullen. The towel had been draped rather precariously around his narrow hips, and looked more provocative than she'd ever imagined it possible of a piece of white towelling.

'Are you in pain?' she asked warily, putting down the knife, worried by the fact that he was hardly breathing.

'Exhausted. I need your help,' he whispered raggedly.

With great caution, she considered him. He certainly looked shattered—but wouldn't a hunky guy like him take a ducking in his stride? 'What do you want?' she asked slowly.

He staggered over to the chair and sat down heavily, his legs definitely wobbling and out of control. But the muscles in his back had rippled beautifully, and she frowned at the conflicting impressions. He hitched up the towel a little, then his hands listlessly attempted to rub at his thighs. He gave up.

'Dammit!' he muttered hoarsely. 'Shock...delayed...' He put his face in his hands and when he drew them away she saw that they were trembling and the eyes which met hers were despairing. 'Look at the state I'm in!' he said, appalled. 'It's humiliating! If my friends could see me...'

Pushing away the quick and uncharitable thought that he couldn't possibly have friends, Suzy began to think he wasn't pretending to be exhausted after all. His shame at being helpless certainly fitted if he was as egocentric and macho as she thought.

'You'll perk up in a minute.'

'I thought I was going to die.' His horrified eyes held hers. 'All my life flashed before me. God, it was terrible!'

'Yes. I imagine your life would be,' she said drily, deliberately fighting the urge to go over and console him. 'Awful to relive all one's sins before they've been forgiven.'

His mouth crimped briefly, then he passed a hand over his forehead, pushing back the dripping waves. 'Everything suddenly hit me forcibly while I was in the shower. I might be lying at the bottom of that canal, bleeding to death, mangled by the hull, the propeller... God, what a horrible way to go!'

She stared at him mutely, her vivid imagination picturing his magnificent body, torn, bloodied... He sat there like a zombie, glistening wet, staring blindly into space.

Her heart was too tender for her own good. She wanted to run and clutch him in her arms. Her stupidity apparently knew no bounds.

'You must dry yourself quickly and wrap up in a dry blanket,' she said with a frown, still holding back. She didn't want to feel sorry for him.

He shook a heavy head. 'Can't. No energy. Strength gone.' He raised pleading, liquid velvet eyes, a shudder making his muscles shimmer, fascinating Suzy with the way they moved. 'I'm so cold. Cold to my bones. Reaction, I suppose. I—I need help. Lord,' he muttered bitterly. 'I loathe being so feeble, but...' The shudder shimmied through him again. 'Please... Dry me?' he asked with the utmost reluctance.

She had to admit that he looked utterly dejected, stripped of his male arrogance and surly aggression. With a resigned sigh, Suzy collected another towel. Few women could have resisted his imploring eyes and defenceless state. Even if it was the helplessness of a trussed tiger. Standing behind him, she began to rough up his hair briskly, then continued more gently when he groaned at her vigour. But the way he moved his head obligingly for her betrayed the fact that other women had done this small service for him, and Suzy felt an irritated twinge of resentment.

Gradually, however, the warmth of the fire, the intimacy of the situation and her task brought back memories which drove away her annoyance. 'It's like drying the kids at the children's home,' she said huskily, past images softening her voice.

'Sounds bloody.'

'Oh, no!' she said, gently patting his face dry. 'It was terrific. I used to help with the toddlers. They were awfully sweet. All pink and soft and tickly.'

'You like kids?'

Her hand stilled for a moment and then carried on. 'Very much,' she said in a low tone, lost in her own thoughts.

To her consternation, she discovered a few moments later that she was still delicately stroking his face with the towel. And he had tipped his head back a little, leaning weakly against her diaphragm as if he was taking a sensual pleasure in her touch. Hardening her heart, she clamped one hand on his jaw and dried his neck hard. He had the sinews of an ox.

'I'm grateful to you,' he said huskily. Suzy worked silently on his collar-bone. 'Glad you were in the spot. Ignore my bad temper earlier. I was furious with those two idiots. You were around so I ranted a bit at you. I shouldn't have taken it out on you, I know. I had to let off steam at someone.'

She gentled her touch, her body less tense as she sensed the difference in the atmosphere between them. It seemed that he'd thought it over and decided she wasn't involved. A flood of relief washed over her. She could relax.

'It's OK,' she said warmly, rubbing the nape of his neck. His hair was thick, and as vigorous as she imagined he was, when he was operating at full throttle. The locks curled into a neat jet-black curve on the tanned skin. 'I'm glad I could help,' she added truthfully. Glad because it put her in a strong position. He owed her something.

'You oughtn't to be walking the streets at night,' he said with a frown. 'It's not safe for a woman as beautiful as you.'

The husky voice was leading somewhere. The eternal equation; flattery plus the late hour plus a half-naked man equals seduction. He had another think coming. He could practise mathematics in someone else's flat.

'You don't know Venice very well, do you? It's very safe,' she replied, sawing the towel across his well-developed shoulders and upper back, and getting rid of her longing to thump him. And, she had to admit, the need to touch the flawless skin with her fingers. 'It's probably the safest city in the world. Women don't get raped or mugged.'

'So there isn't much call for detective work, then?' he commented idly over his shoulder.

Her hands stopped for a split second and, to cover up her surprise, she pushed him forwards with a rough movement so that his massive back was more accessible. He drew in his breath sharply when his body folded, and she remembered with a slightly guilty feeling that his ribs were bruised.

'Sorry. Detectives? I wouldn't know,' she said innocently, searching for a way to be as truthful as possible. She kicked herself for relaxing her guard. Every time she thought she was free from suspicion he slid in a sneaky question. 'I'm a cook, not a crook. Cooks don't get involved in crime.' She laughed. 'Agatha Christie has passed me by.'

Her nerves were jumping and she thought back over the last couple of days. He couldn't have seen her following him. She'd taken elaborate precautions, wearing a variety of insignificant outfits.

'I think I've passed you by, too,' he said earnestly. 'I'm sure I've seen you somewhere recently.'

'Quite likely!' she laughed, forcing gaiety. 'It's a tiny city. In a place two miles by one, you're bound to bump into your friends ten times a day and see strangers so often that they seem familiar. I dash here and there——'

'Cooking for street parties? Pizzas on the move?' he murmured.

'No! I mean I'm always going from one place to another.' Her hands moved thoughtfully over the worryingly developed muscles of his biceps. 'I've washed up all the way from the *Zattere* to the *Ospedale*—oh, I suppose you don't know what I'm talking about,' she said, deciding to tackle him head-on. In that case, she'd need to see his reactions. She moved to turn the fire down a little. Kneeling in front of him and daringly deciding to leave her skirt so that she showed a couple of inches of thigh above the knee, to divert him, she reached forwards to dry his chest. 'You tourists never go further than St Mark's and Rialto,' she chided. 'How much do you know about Venice?'

'Guidebook stuff.' His eyes held hers in a hard, knowing stare. 'Let me see. A city of decadent grandeur, secretive deals, bribery and corruption, exorbitantly high prices——'

'You've been reading the wrong books,' she frowned. Venice was wonderful, and she wouldn't have it criticised. He shrugged non-committally. 'You speak a bit of Italian, don't you?' she asked casually, remembering his call for help had been in English at first. Italian wasn't his instinctive language. That had been a surprise.

'A bit. I come from Switzerland.' His eyes bored into hers, gauging her reaction as if Switzerland should be significant to her, but it wasn't.

'That explains your good English,' she smiled. He nodded his head, faintly amused. 'How long are you here for?'

'As long as it takes,' he said softly.

Suzy felt the hairs rising on the back of her neck. She patted his foot and he obediently lifted it on to her knee. But all the while her mind was teeming with ideas to stay close to him. Dangerous, perhaps. But interesting. Exciting. Her eyes sparkled like dewy grass.

'A lovely long holiday! How lucky you are. Won't your boss mind?' she asked, cocking her head up with an appealing tilt to it.

'I'm freelance. I do as I please.'

'Freelance!' she said admiringly. 'What job would that be?'

He paused, his eyes mocking. 'I take people's money from them.'

She gulped. 'Oh.' He was deliberately *admitting* he was a blackmailer. That was alarming. 'Like a bank does,' she said a little breathily.

His mouth twitched in amusement. 'Like a bank,' he agreed in a voice as smooth as honey. 'You know Venice,' he said idly, changing the subject. 'Why don't you show me around? Give me a good time?'

With infinite deliberation, his hand reached out to push back the heavily falling waves which hid her face from view. It was a highly erotic gesture, and Suzy's stomach constricted at the tingle which curled sharply inside her as his fingers lightly pushed into her warm scalp and caressed the skin behind her ear.

His earlier grappling technique had been modified, to her alarm. This was more dangerous. He was smiling gently, the upward curve of his mouth highly sensual.

Waves of sexual energy flowed from his body, disconcerting her. He was revving up to make a pass. Suzy
gave a hasty flash of the towel over his calves and handed
it over to him.

'Why not?' she smiled, concealing the mixture of
nerves and delight churning around inside her. They'd
meet again. She'd have a chance to beat him at his own
game. She'd never failed in an assignment yet. The
Contessa wanted to know everything about him, and he
was innocently handing himself to her on a plate. 'Look,
see if you can finish off drying yourself. I'd better get
on with the meal.'

'Pretty little thing,' he murmured, chucking her under
the chin.

Suzy simpered and seethed. That did it! She wouldn't
let him get away with that. He needed bringing to book.
And, of course, he knew an embarrassing secret, as yet
unknown to her, which terrified the Contessa Flavia and
her son, Prince Guido Moroschini. That alone would
keep her hard on his trail.

Seductive music filled the room. Suzy frowned at the
chilli pepper she was de-seeding, her body unac-
countably tense. Her edginess and her scorn went up
two notches as a honey-voiced contralto crooned a gentle
love-song on the radio and she heard the man plumping
up the pillows. It sounded unnervingly intimate. Did he
have a few surprises coming!

'Don't mind if I get in your bed to keep warm, do
you?' he murmured throatily, his voice reverberating in
the small space.

The direct approach. Unsubtle, blundering. 'Not in
the least,' she said airily. She strained for the sound of
the sheets, the slide of a body, and realised she was for-
getting to breathe. When she did, it was hard and rapid.
Her knife cut viciously through the defenceless pepper,
her mind racing.

'Mmm. Heaven. Nothing like bed, after a hard day, is there? I feel better already. What's your name?' he asked lazily.

'Suzy Carlini.'

'Hello, Suzy Carlini.'

She smiled politely over her shoulder. The smile faltered a little. He was lounging back against the pillows, his bare, muscled arms behind his head, totally at ease, as if he was used to being in strange women's beds. All right, so he had a gorgeous physique, she thought sourly. But he was as black as canal mud inside. Those dark, voracious eyes were lethal weapons.

'Fiorenzo Veronese,' he murmured in a slow drawl.

She knew that. His lethal weapons found their target and threatened her with first-degree burns. She slid back a flirty look, confident in her ability to withstand villainous blackmailers. 'That's Italian. You talk like a Surrey stockbroker,' she laughed, aware that she was having to keep a check on her pounding pulses. And that added to the danger, the excitement.

He smiled enigmatically and said nothing, other than what he was saying with his eloquent eyes. Come here, they said. Come and have the time of your life. Suzy's mouth twitched. He had one thing on his mind, and wasn't going to let her questions get in his way.

Frustrated, she turned back to the chicken left-overs. He was going to be a hard nut to crack. It was an extraordinary situation. Perhaps she was stupid to be playing this game, considering the awe with which the Contessa spoke of him. 'Merciless'. 'Malevolent'. But it was a fantastic challenge. Preoccupied with her apprehension, Suzy absently tossed back her hair, which had fallen over her shoulders.

He groaned, and every inch of her responded by tensing expectantly. She had to consciously make herself continue to prepare the meal as if she hadn't heard. He groaned again.

'Suzy,' he said huskily. 'Can you do something about this bruise? Every time I breathe it hurts like hell where you slammed that plank into me.'

Her heart thudded. She knew that tone of voice. He was intending to try his luck and make that pass. Or more—hoping to score a goal. She'd need a bit of nifty work in defence to get out of this yet keep him sweet. She smiled ruefully. He was quite something! How energetic and virile would he be when he *wasn't* exhausted, recovering from shock and suffering from bruises?

Doctors and nurses. Oh, lord! How incredibly obvious! Jauntily, she walked over, poker-faced, bottle and cotton wool in her hand, wishing she could deliver the ultimate put-down and tell him he didn't appeal. Unfortunately, somehow she had to refuse him without wounding his manly pride. She must learn more about him—but not physically. She'd seen enough of him to know instinctively that he'd be very persuasive, very persistent, very *active*.

Slowly he drew back the covers from his torso, his dark, steady eyes smouldering intensely at her. God, she loathed men like him! Arrogant sexual adventurers... There was a fiery elation in the depths of his eyes, an intense satisfaction that was arrantly male, and, try as she might, she couldn't stop herself from responding to the dizzying excitement of combat. He was after her body and wouldn't care how he got it. She was going to outwit him. Her eyes met his steadily, smiling, concealing her intentions.

'Here,' she said, holding the witch-hazel at arm's length.

'Come here,' he invited.

'We'll eat first,' she said pleasantly.

'You should never eat first. Never take the edge off your hunger.' There was a predatory gleam in his eyes, as if he'd honed in on his prey and wasn't going to let it get away.

'You need a little time to get your strength up,' she stated sweetly.

'It's up.'

She flushed at his suggestively raised eyebrow. 'Not enough for me, Fiorenzo,' she husked. 'I need one hundred per cent effort.'

His mouth quirked, the velvet eyes glowed. 'So do I,' he said with a muted growl. 'Come here!'

'Oh!' She slapped her hand on her stomach and looked embarrassed. 'Did you hear that? My stomach's rumbling something awful! I'll go and——'

'Aren't you going to play?' he asked softly.

She contemplated his avidly greedy face, the blatant carnality, the slumbering strength. If she had any sense, she'd know that a graceful withdrawal would be more sensible than trying to keep this man at arm's length.

'With a rumbling stomach?' she laughed, sounding apologetic.

'Shame,' he grinned. The grin hid his intention. He moved like lightning, his arm flashing out, his fingers curling around her wrist and clamping together like an iron band. Suzy's eyes flashed to his and she lifted a severe eyebrow at him in warning.

'Risotto.' Suzy lifted her chin, ready to do battle.

He smiled again. Slowly. His hand stroked the rich sheen of his jaw speculatively, gently tracing the sullen bruise. 'Oh, women always like to play hard to get. They say "no" when they mean "yes".' His eyes mocked the brief flare of anger that crossed her face. 'Come on, Suzy, do your womanly bit. Soothe my hurt,' he coaxed in a gentle, persuasive voice. 'That's what you women are best at. What you're really for. To administer to...*all* men's needs.'

So that was the kind of man he was. To hide her cold dislike, Suzy flipped her eyes to the ceiling in mock horror. 'God, that's corny,' she teased. 'I'm cooking,' she said, aghast that her voice shook.

'So am I,' he said tensely. 'Feel.'

The bottle of witch-hazel was unpeeled from her grasp by ruthless fingers which would have broken her fist if she hadn't released her hold. She was about to move and adjust her body to throw him, but he quickly dropped the bottle to the floor and yanked her closer, putting pressure on her hand that made her yelp.

'Fiorenzo——!'

'I'm not hurting, am I? Sometimes I forget my own strength,' he laughed apologetically. But his eyes hardened, and she was jerked violently forwards as he thudded back on to the pillows and she fell heavily to lie full-length across him. He grunted as she bounced on his ribs, but he wasn't daunted.

'Feel,' he said thickly, his lashes lowering with a brooding look. 'Feel me. Touch me. I'm hot. Burning. Have I a fever, Suzy? Or is it you?'

Before she knew what was happening, his hand was cradling the back of her head, bringing it down to his mouth, and she was being ferociously, triumphantly kissed. He groaned and winced at the pain it brought his bruised jaw, but kept kissing. Thoroughly. Warmth flooded through her as his marauding mouth moved over her softening lips. Suzy felt his arms bind to her like coiling steel. She tried to work out some way of evading him, but her brain went soft and woolly. With the heat of his body and the knowledge that he was virtually naked beneath the sheets came a fear that struck her stupid.

She wrenched her lips from his. 'What—what are you doing?' she breathed, aghast. It was perfectly obvious what he was doing. Winning.

'Returning a favour. I want to give you something in return for what you've done. I have little money,' he said softly. 'I have nothing to give you as thanks, except...' He contemplated her parted lips hungrily and, to her dismay, Suzy felt an overwhelming shaft of pure answering need slice through her, echoed by the flare in his smoky eyes. 'Women say I'm good,' he husked. 'Passionate. Earthy as a gypsy, energetic as a bull. Let me show you, amuse you. My "thank you".'

'Please,' Suzy protested, stunned by his arrogant assumptions. 'You may be in my debt, but heaven forbid that you should be forced to sell your honour!'

There was a twitching at the corner of his mobile mouth, and she thought he was struggling not to laugh, but finally the laughter broke through and he threw his head back and roared, releasing the tension which had built up between them.

'Not many women can make me laugh.' He smiled wrly. 'Nor men, for that matter. You're a very quick-tongued, wicked woman, Suzy Carlini.' He grinned in delight.

'That's me,' she said cheerfully. Her anxiety subsided, and she was thankful that the difficult moment was over. Unfortunately, however, he hadn't finished with her. A lazy desire warmed his eyes, and she drew back warily, but he reached out and roughly hauled her wriggling body back on to the bed beside him, his hands sliding up her arms, and seduction in every inch of his sensual face.

'No,' she said firmly.

'I adore bad women,' he growled, gazing teasingly at her.

'I'm not *that* wicked!' she croaked, staring into his black wrecker's eyes, wondering if she ought to slug him.

'You soon will be,' he promised, desire thickening his voice. 'Wait till I show you what I learned in Hong Kong!'

Mesmerised, she watched as his finger lifted to test the softness of her pink mouth, and for the life of her she couldn't understand why the world had begun to move with the consistency of treacle.

She didn't like blundering men. But... this was suddenly not blundering. His lightly drifting finger hypnotised her into immobility, bringing a liquid weakness to her body. The tension had risen again, now as thick and enveloping as a Venetian fog, and far more dangerous, because the exploration of his finger had begun to feel alarmingly like the caress of a lover.

Suzy opened her mouth with a supreme effort, intending to rebuke him, since she was clean out of witticisms. But her throat was too dry, and no sound would emerge. She tensed a knee, ready; but, forestalling her thrust to his groin, Fiorenzo's leg crooked around her knee, the side of his foot rhythmically massaging the satiny back of her leg, the whole of his body urgent, poised, ready.

She swallowed hard. 'Naughty,' she husked indulgently, with a little laugh of disapproval. Hong Kong had a lot to answer for, she thought ruefully. 'I want my supper.'

And then she'd arm herself with a battery of knives. And forks. And the mincer.

'Sorry. Can't wait,' he drawled lazily. 'I'm hungry *now*.'

Roughly his strong thumb tilted up her small chin, and she was gazing straight into the compelling black infinity of his eyes, his breath softly, deliberately whispering over her sensitised skin, the music of a golden aria washing over her and sending her senses spinning into orbit.

'No,' she protested tremulously, into his mouth. This wasn't in the script she'd written. Her body wasn't supposed to give in without a battle. Her fluttering hands found his chest and pushed.

The muscles tensed, resisting her. His plundering mouth became hard and grim, the pressure relentless on her lips, as if he had such a savage hunger that only violence would satisfy it.

'Don't be too hard to get,' he growled, his eyes flashing with excitement. 'You'll torment me so much that I might inadvertently hurt you in my frustration.' He licked his lips lasciviously, and Suzy's eyes rounded.

'Hurt me?' she whispered, her heart thudding. Was that a blatant threat?

'It's your fault. Your denial is arousing me. Your body, your mouth, the way you move, is highly erotic.' His voice sounded thick with need, and Suzy tried to swallow away the fear that clogged her throat. 'I want you. God . . . the very idea excites me.'

'Fio——' Her squeaky voice gave out at the savage glow of his eyes. This was *definitely* not in the script. She'd been in a light comedy, he was moving into *Rambo II*.

Hauling her on top of him, ruthlessly ignoring her gasp of complaint, he pinioned her so skilfully that he was able to kiss her unhindered and she was a complete prisoner, unable to move, utterly helpless. Like a relentless storm, his kisses rained down, hot, fierce, grinding into her mouth, demanding a response from her. She gritted her teeth hard and went as stiff as a board.

'Oh, the challenge,' he said with a low laugh. 'You bitch. You know what I like! A woman who resists me! I can barely control myself! You're teasing me!'

'N—o!' she said, the word cracking into two syllables. 'I don't——'

He had covered her mouth with his, and his legs had kicked away the sheet totally to twine lithely around hers, the shock of his hot, muscled thighs and the hard line of his hip making her whole body grow rigid with tension till she thought she would snap like a brittle stick in his arms.

As she moaned with anger low in her throat, he gave a deep, sexual growl and enclosed her lower lip with his teeth, softly savouring it, tugging, sucking. Suzy wondered hazily why that should be so infinitely exciting when she hated him so much, why small thrills were chasing around her breasts. She closed her eyes and kept herself unresponsive. Only Mario had ever kissed her so intimately—and then never so...so earthily, like a hungry animal.

The kisses grew sultry, slow, exploring, and she forgot his rough handling in the new delicacy of touch. His tongue stabbed at the centre of her compressed lips, and a *frisson* ran through both their bodies at the same time, as if linking them. Suzy felt herself wavering beneath his infinitely sweet mouth and raiding, skilful fingers.

Danger, excitement...now she had that. Was loving it—and hating herself for being so aroused by primitive feelings, aware of the surging heat between them, their mutual panting, flashing eyes, bared teeth. Something wild and carnal inside her wanted to yell at him, tear out his hair, trade kiss for kiss. She felt bewildered by the storm of feeling he'd aroused inside her. It was awful.

She loathed him because he'd made her want his savage passion. It appalled her that she could be attracted to a man living on the edge of civilisation, daring to defy the law, risking all. He was dragging her down to his level. To the gutter. She wouldn't succumb, she *wouldn't*!

'Have fun,' he growled. 'Fight me!'

She knew that that was what he wanted, and that it would arouse him. So she held herself like a rigid statue in his loathsome embrace. But she was in a no-win situation. For he was taking advantage of her acquiescence. Fiorenzo's body shifted and he lifted her a little so that she could feel the movement of her nipples against his naked chest. They sprang into life, hardening, demanding to be touched, shaming her with their need.

Suzy whimpered in distress—or pleasure, she wasn't sure—when he moved sensually beneath her, and then, with a small mocking laugh, he rolled over, taking her with him, lifting her arms above her head and letting his head slowly angle downwards, the slow simmer of his eyes rendering her quite speechless.

She remembered dimly that she could flatten any man if she wanted to. She didn't have to lie there, waiting for his assault. In desperation she worked out her options. An ankle-flip. It would wind him if... There was a chuckle in her ear. Although all she had done was to flex her ankle, ready to toss him over, by some extraordinary fluke he was ready for her movement and she found herself flat on her back again.

'Lie back and enjoy it, Green Eyes,' he said maliciously. 'Your toes are curling. Join them; let your whole body go.'

'They're not!' she husked, incensed with him—and herself, finding her voice at last. Cracked, shaky, but serviceable.

'They damn well are,' he murmured.

She tried to straighten her toes, and he laughed softly, triumphantly, with that cock-sure male confidence which made her want to throttle him. 'No!' she raged.

To her utter amazement, he pushed her away. 'Oh, dear. It seems,' he said lazily, his eyes burning into hers, 'that I may have misinterpreted your reason for inviting me up.'

Relief flooded through every tense muscle. 'You have. You take some persuading,' she muttered.

'Well, at least I know how far you'll go,' he said silkily. Suzy sensed a hidden meaning behind his words, and looked at him with wary eyes. 'Or is it part of your plan to keep me panting for more?'

Warning bells sounded in her head. She lifted her lustrous green eyes limpidly to his. 'Please!' she protested. 'I'm not a tease. I understand now that you thought I was asking you to my flat to—to get better acquainted. You've realised your mistake. So shall we settle for a nice risotto?' she suggested with an inane smile, lifting herself cautiously away from him.

'Anything to take my mind off what I wanted to do,' he growled.

His hand trailed to her breast and covered it boldly. She gave a husky, feminine laugh. And then gasped, offended by his impudent finger which had flicked the tip of her breast and made her rock with unexpected, unwanted pleasure.

'I'll have you,' he murmured, with a sinister twist to his mouth. He turned it into a half-smile of promise that seemed utterly chilling to her heightened senses. 'Sooner or later. I always get what I want.'

CHAPTER THREE

'How masterful you are,' murmured Suzy with a wide-eyed admiration that fooled neither of them. Fiorenzo laughed, and she got up gracefully and continued to prepare the meal, humming to herself to lift her shaken spirits. She ignored the way her hand shook. Nerves, that was all.

'Don't be long,' he said, yawning and stretching. 'I'm beginning to feel sleepy. And I need to build up my strength. For later.'

Suzy made a mental note never to meet him anywhere isolated. She poured oil into a pan and waited for it to heat up.

If it wasn't for the Contessa, she'd turf him out without a second thought. But she owed a debt of gratitude to Flavia Moroschini. Only four months ago, Suzy had been working for an investigation agency in Venice. Prince Guido Moroschini had brought his mother into her office to thank her for tracing the daughter of one of their friends.

She'd been surprised at the time, since it was shortly after Flavia's brother had died in the accident which had left the Contessa paralysed. Somehow, Flavia had discovered Suzy's ambition to set up her own agency, and had let her use a dilapidated building rent-free for her office and apartment. Without the lady's patronage, Suzy's business would have failed. In Venice, it was who you knew, not what you knew, that brought success.

Suzy tipped onion into the pan and added the garlic, lots of it, feeling in charge of the situation once more.

She was good at her job, and had used the Contessa's generous introductions well. Already she had traced a couple of teenagers and healed the family differences, all without a breath of scandal touching the aristocratic families involved. 'A sleuth with sentimental tendencies,' Guido had said.

Her face softened. She had an affection for the brave Contessa, and had become Guido's friend. She wouldn't fail them. Not even if it meant letting this arrogant swine paw her again.

Fiorenzo had known she had been unwillingly aroused. She frowned, wishing she wasn't so emotional. Even in the children's home she had struggled to curb her powerful feelings, knowing that her intense passion would bewilder the sweet Sisters of Charity.

Yet this had meant she'd laid herself open for Mario once she'd left the home. Suzy stared into space, remembering how she'd met him at a dance when she was eighteen. His flamboyant Italian behaviour had been like a breath of fresh air. His passion had equalled hers, though she had gone to him a virgin on their wedding night. And discovered too late that married sex was quick, brutal and unsatisfying.

Her face sobered. Fiorenzo, alone of all men, had caused her body to throb. Or maybe her hormones were telling her it was time she settled down and had babies.

Suzy felt the old pain scissoring away at her insides, and she deliberately forced herself to consider the problem of Fiorenzo. To satisfy her thirst for some kind of action, she planned a spectacular revenge. Prison was too good for him. Boiling in oil... Castration... Her eyes gleamed.

'Right,' she said, dishing up the food. 'Come and get it.'

She flushed, realising what she'd said, and waited for his sexy growl and mocking answer. He was silent. Slowly she turned her head. He was sprawled on the bed fast asleep, one arm flung over his head.

Her eyes brooded on him. She couldn't resist going over to the bed. Startling black, crescent-shaped lashes lay heavily on his cheeks. In repose his mouth was slightly pouting and eminently kissable, the line of his aristocratic nose demanding the stroke of her finger. He smiled in his sleep. That sweet, innocent smile tugged fatally at Suzy's heart, making it beat like an African drum. He had no right to look so harmless or so incredibly handsome.

Irritably she dragged her eyes away and went into the bathroom to investigate his wallet. It contained a little money, but nothing else. No identification, no credit cards, not one thing to give her any clues about him or what he was going to do in Venice. She lifted her head, frowning. That was very odd. She'd have a lot of questions to ask him.

Replacing the wallet in his jacket, she ate a little of the risotto, then prepared for sleep. The massive steel hulls of the boats on the quayside thirty yards away began to clang together as the wind shifted direction. Suzy groaned as she curled up in the armchair. It sounded to her as if she was going to have a disturbed night.

'Morning.'

Still drugged with sleep, Suzy huddled deeper into the armchair. A smell of coffee came to her nose. A hand shook her arm and she pouted. Her lips were covered by a warm mouth. She felt the bristly rasp of five o'clock shadow on her soft skin, and crossly she wrenched herself away, turning in the opposite direction.

'*No*, Mario!' she muttered sulkily. He was insatiable...

'Good grief, I've got a rival!'

Fiorenzo, sounding cold and cynical. Suzy's eyes snapped open and she sat up hurriedly, then put a hand to her throbbing forehead. A steam-hammer was hitting it from the inside.

'Who....? Oh, you,' she said, glaring into Fiorenzo's mocking eyes. With great dignity she wrapped her dressing-gown more securely around her and scrambled out of the twisted blanket. 'I've had a rotten night,' she muttered. 'So you'd better not be one of those chirpy morning men.'

'Met a few, have you?' he asked coolly, looking very rakish with his burgeoning beard.

She gave him a caustic look. 'I feel terrible. How do you feel?' she asked, ignoring his remark.

He put a gentle hand on her brow. 'Sore, but improving,' he assured her, his fingers slipping down and massaging her temple beautifully. His smile lifted the heavy shadows under his eyes, and Suzy wondered if he'd slept badly too. 'I'm looking forward to today.'

'That's more than I can claim,' she muttered irritably, throwing off his hand and going into the bathroom. When she came back, dressed in a warm red wool dress, there was a gorgeous smell of hot pastries. 'Where did they come from? I usually go to a bar for breakfast,' she said grumpily, not keen on intimate meals with him when her mind was less than razor-sharp.

'I got someone to do that for me.'

She looked him up and down and raised an arching eyebrow. He was wearing a sheet. He grinned, and she blinked at the way it infused his face with vitality. But not his eyes, she thought with a frown. They were untouched, chilled by a glacial light.

'It's the maid's day off,' she said sarcastically. 'Who did you ask?'

'I knocked on the doors below this flat, but no one seemed to be at home——'

'There's only me here,' she interrupted impatiently, hoping she'd locked her office up securely. 'Don't say you went out like that?'

'Good lord, no!' he drawled. 'Too cold. I was tidying up the flat for you——'

'You were *what*?' Suzy asked in alarm, her eyes darting around the room. Her heart slammed in her chest at the possibility that he might find something incriminating...a letter-head... She tried to remember what was in the room and was almost certain that there was nothing to give her away.

His expressive mouth curled up at the corners with pleasure. 'Thought you'd be surprised,' he said in a self-satisfied voice. 'Anyway, I found a basket with a long rope on it. I realised it was what people in high buildings use to drop out of the window for the postman,' he explained. 'Awfully quaint. *So*, I lowered it out of the window and spoke charmingly to a little old lady walking by, saying my clothes had been taken away by my jealous mistress and I was hungry. Had to smear on the old magnetism a bit,' he murmured.

Suzy wanted to smack his smug face. 'Are you saying she simply trotted off and bought you pastries?' she said in disbelief.

'Please! This is Venice! Everything at a price, everyone can be bought, isn't that right?' he asked softly. Suzy's eyes narrowed, and he opened his hands in an expressive shrug. 'I dug my wallet out of my jacket,' he said, his dark eyes intent on her pale face, 'and extracted some money. She saw the chance to make a quick buck and scuttled to the bakery to diddle me out of the change.'

Suzy was incensed. 'You—you—— Oh!' she exploded. 'How could you? I live in this neighbourhood! Everyone will know you've been up here——'

'Mario seemed to have been welcome,' he remarked drily.

'He was my husband,' she said tightly. 'And that was in Naples five years ago, and I'm not married to him any longer.'

'Five years, eh?' He gave her a knowing wink. 'That explains it. Last night it got a bit heated back there at one stage, didn't it?'

Suzy glowered at him. She knew perfectly well what he was getting at. 'That's not very gentlemanly,' she said coldly.

'Well, there you go. A number of people would be quick to tell you that I'm not a gentleman,' he said with a cynical lift to his sculpted mouth. He gave her a crooked grin. 'The pastries are getting cold. It would be a shame to waste them.'

His logic was faultless. It was his ethics which left a lot to be desired. Suzy inhaled deeply and then exhaled. 'You're in high spirits this morning,' she grumbled.

'I am. My accident last night gave me a metaphorical kick in the pants. It needs a shock like that sometimes, doesn't it? I'm going to take life by the throat and shake it.'

It might be a trick of the light, but his eyes appeared to be aimed directly at *her* throat. Suzy wondered what he was going to do. She ought to quiz him, but felt so tired. Food might help. She sat down at the table and demolished her fair share of pastries, fending off his attempts at conversation with a few well-aimed scowls while she hatched a plan.

Pretending she didn't know where he lived, she persuaded him to let her have his keys. She'd been surprised how easy it had been to coax him. His apartment was close and she quickly reached it, searching the small flat carefully. There was nothing incriminating, no evidence of any papers or photographs—and only a small sailbag which had obviously contained the few clothes he'd brought. In fact, she thought, as she made her way back with the sailbag full of warm clothes, it was almost as if he was deliberately trying to be anonymous.

She looked at him suspiciously when she returned, but he was still at the table drinking coffee where she'd left him, stretched out in his chair like a lord, and with a plateful of pastry crumbs before him. The dirty dishes from the night before were still unwashed; Fiorenzo evidently didn't believe in doing domestic chores. She'd chuck him out and get some sleep before tackling the day.

'If you'd dress,' she said pleasantly, 'I can get to work.'

He stretched like a big, lazy lion. 'It's early. Surely you don't have to start yet?'

'Awful, isn't it? I have to shop in Rialto before all the best bargains have gone,' she improvised. 'So——'

'I can help,' he said, unravelling the sheet around him eagerly. Suzy hastily turned her back. He had no hesitation in stripping in front of women, she thought sourly. He probably did it every day. 'I can carry your bags for you.'

'I wouldn't put you to all that trouble. I'll be going on after the shopping to do a cooking job,' she lied in desperation, stacking the dishes. Her head was so bad that she couldn't play 'seductive Suzy', and she certainly had no stamina for a whole morning of innuendo and trying to keep one step ahead of him.

'No bother at all.' He heaved a sigh. 'In fact, I want to do something——' He held up his hand at her opening mouth. 'Yes, I know I offered you a little roll in the hay, and it's not my fault we're both frustrated. All in all, I've been a hell of a nuisance. That mess in your bathroom...my bad temper...I can't tell you how rotten I feel, Suzy. I wanted to murder everyone in sight, especially whoever set me up.' His diamond eyes glinted at her. 'You see, I haven't exactly enjoyed myself in Venice since I arrived, and was feeling sour.'

She thought of the way he'd wandered around aimlessly. She hadn't enjoyed following him, either. Dragging round streets, wandering into every church he came across... Most peculiar. 'You don't need to apologise——' she began.

He shrugged his shoulders Italian-style. 'I do. I want to do something positive...' He smiled, but Suzy had the impression that the smile was for him, not her. 'In return for *everything* you've done for me. You should wear gloves,' he finished abruptly.

Startled, Suzy took a moment before she realised what he was talking about. She had plunged her hands back into the soapy water. He'd known her for five minutes, and was already bossing her around. 'I loathe them,' she said fervently. 'They make my hands sweat. I like to feel things when——'

'So do I,' he agreed enthusiastically.

'Down, Fido,' she ordered with a little chuckle, cutting him to size.

'There I go again,' he sighed, picking up a tea-towel, to her surprise. 'Making a nuisance of myself. I'm going to break the habit of a lifetime and dry up, to show you I'm a reformed man. I would like to make amends. Something more exciting than wielding a tea-towel? Stand you lunch, dinner——?'

Suzy knew she ought to arrange to see him again. When she was feeling tough and could choose somewhere like the middle of St Mark's basilica, where he'd have to keep his hands to himself. She handed him a plate and pretended to be deciding.

'Look, you'd hate shopping, a macho man like you. All that haggling in the fish market, and choosing sprouts. So unmanly!' she murmured. 'And I'm not very good company today, what with one thing and another. Perhaps lunch sometime, if you like.'

They argued. He was adamant and stubborn, saying he had to go in the direction of Rialto that morning anyway. Unable to refuse without being too obvious, she reluctantly agreed to let him carry her bags.

Inwardly she was raging. It would be a waste of money and a waste of energy. It meant that she'd have to come all the way back to her apartment with food she didn't even want, then almost retrace her steps to meet the Contessa at eleven to present her report. She'd have fallen arches by the time she finished this assignment.

'Why not lunch today? I'm bored,' he complained. 'You can tell that. I've never sunk to making a date shopping in a market before.'

Suzy bit back a scornful comment. No one could be bored in Venice. And it wasn't a date. 'Shame Venice isn't your cup of tea. I suppose you'll be going home sooner than you thought,' she said sympathetically. 'I really can't make lunch today. I have a party tonight I must prepare for. Look, we'd better go. I must see if I've got enough money.' She felt irritated that he'd inconvenienced her again, and wondered how little she could buy without raising his suspicions. Perhaps she could put it down to expenses in the course of her duties.

'I can lend you some money if you like,' he offered. 'That is, if you haven't already taken my board and lodging from my wallet,' he added with an easy laugh.

Her eyes narrowed. 'I don't take money from men,' she said, bristling.

'I was joking. I know it's all there. I counted it when I paid for the pastries,' he replied evenly. 'I was rather glad to find it still in my jacket, though. As a matter of fact, I thought my wallet had been lost last night.'

'Last night?' she queried in a rather high voice, her pulses racing at his unpleasant smile.

Fiorenzo lifted a puzzled eyebrow. 'Why, yes. When I flung myself full length in the canal.'

Suzy's hand shook as she tucked wisps of hair behind her ear. He helped her. She smiled weakly and reached for her coat. He helped her. She felt like a mouse, being played by a cat. But he couldn't be doing it deliberately, could he? With a sinking feeling, Suzy knew she had to keep up her performance that morning to put him off the scent. And all she wanted was to crawl into bed and sleep.

'Headache bad?' he asked sympathetically.

She nodded. He massaged her temples again, and she stood there, letting him, finding the gentle rhythm of his surprisingly delicate fingers very soothing. Her eyes closed. God, she was tired! He kissed her. After a moment's hesitation, she put her arms around his neck and joined in.

She had to stay friendly with him. His lips were gentle and sweet without any threat, and he held her lightly by the shoulders. Before any passion flared between them, his mouth drew away and she found herself actually feeling sorry.

'You ought to market that cure,' she smiled ruefully.

A warmth filled his eyes and then was extinguished by the guarded expression he protected himself with. She touched his arm, detaining him. 'I'm sorry if I was jittery with you at any time last night,' she said. 'It was a bit unnerving for me.'

'Yes. I suppose it was.'

His tone gave nothing away at all. Coolly he opened the door, and Suzy knew he was still wary of her. Intentionally she walked close to Fiorenzo as they crossed the bridge by the Arsenale. No one ever died of being groped, she told herself. The end justified the means.

'Look,' she said, pointing to the lion-guarded entrance to the docks. 'The old shipyard. It used to be the biggest in the world. Sad that it's almost derelict, isn't it? Loads of places in Venice are. Especially the palaces,' she said, leading the conversation to where she wanted it to go. Her arm slipped into his in a friendly, confiding manner.

He looked down at her cynically. 'That's probably because the owners have spent all their money on bribing officials,' he remarked.

'It's not really corruption. Would you stand in a bank queue if you had a contact who'd get you to the front?'

His lip curled in contempt. 'Sounds immoral.'

'No, it's different. That's the way we do things here. We call it oiling the wheels,' she explained, as they watched a mad tourist, draped in cloak and mask, battling against the elements. Fiorenzo smiled, and the openness of his face as he dropped his guard for that moment quite took her breath away.

'He's crazy.' Fiorenzo's amused eyes followed the tourist as he stubbornly celebrated Carnival. 'Damned if I'd go sightseeing in this weather.'

Suzy felt his body stiffen, and she knew he'd caught himself making a gaffe. So he hadn't been sightseeing. What, then? Why had he trailed around the streets and churches? He pulled her close, so that her thigh lined up against his and his arm curved around her waist, and she found it difficult to keep her train of thought. It occurred to her that he was manhandling her deliberately.

'It's popular by the Arsenale in autumn,' she said, persevering with her line of conversation. 'This is quite a smart place to come. The aristocracy stroll here to remind themselves how they made their money, by trade with the Orient. So you can spend the autumn falling over counts and princes, contessas...'

She watched him from beneath her lashes. He didn't even blink. He had an unnerving self-control.

'They made money from shipbuilding and trade?' he queried as they moved away. Suzy hung on to him possessively. 'I thought they all got wealthy from those glass factories on Murano.'

'Some did. The Moroschini family, for instance, before they became merchant princes as well.' Fiorenzo never even checked his stride or tensed a muscle. Suzy was surprised at how cool he was.

'And the others?' he asked quietly.

'They were kings of the sea, making a quick buck by hiring galleys out to the Crusaders and milking them for all they were worth,' she smiled. 'Half of Europe must have been in Venice's debt. Crafty lot, the Venetians.'

'So I've discovered,' he said drily.

'Oh, dear. You've been fleeced?' she enquired, giving him a sickly sympathetic look.

It was like staring at solid ice. His hard profile briefly turned to her, to transfix her with expressionless black eyes. 'Sort of,' he replied, his mouth grim. 'I was relieved of something that was mine. But I know how to remedy that.'

She felt waves of hostility coming from him, and cuddled close. 'Good for you. What are you going to do?' she asked curiously.

'Take what is mine by force. And flatten anyone who stands in my way.'

'Oh, my!' she gushed admiringly, hugging his arm. 'Just like Rambo!'

He flung her a cynical look. 'I believe in using a sledge-hammer to crack a nut,' he said softly as they came out on to the Riva degli Schiavoni, the quayside along the curve of St. Mark's basin. 'That way, you crack the nut first time and get to have what you want from it.' The threat was crystal-clear. His arm hauled her harder into his body with an arrogant possession. 'Cold, isn't it?' he said disarmingly as an involuntary shiver ran through her.

'Freezing,' she agreed in as normal a tone as she could manage. 'How lovely I've got you to keep me warm,' she simpered. His arm clamped her to his thigh like a vice. 'Gently,' she smiled through her discomfort. 'You could crack my ribs.'

'Yes,' he acknowledged, 'I suppose I could.' He relieved the pressure by a millimetre. 'I get very passionate about what is mine and what I want. As I said, I do like to have my own way.'

'So do I,' she muttered, her chin determined.

'But I always succeed, because I don't care how I get it,' he said, and the controlled violence in his whole body made Suzy's stomach churn with fear. His face darkened. 'My aunt once called me a psychopath.'

Suzy gulped. She didn't like what she was hearing. The Contessa had warned her how lethal this man was. She hurried him to the *vaporetto* stop, desperately thinking of a way to lighten up the conversation, and wishing the ordeal of the morning were already over.

'We get the water-bus here. It's called the *accelerato*, but don't let that fool you.' She flicked a waveringly bright smile at his impassive face. 'It stops at every single landing stage on both banks of the Grand Canal,' she said nervously. 'Isn't that just typical?'

Fiorenzo's mouth twitched, but he said nothing, and she led him on to the lurching pontoon, staring out at the grey, choppy lagoon and waiting for the boat to arrive from the island. They boarded the boat and cosily, like any courting couple, huddled together in the cabin of the water-bus.

He seemed very quiet. Suzy dutifully pointed out the sights as the water-bus forged determinedly past the Salute church and into the Grand Canal. She tried to be bright and vaguely alluring. His right hand absently curved around her waist. The other massaged her knee enthusiastically. Suzy stuck it out and coped by expressing enormous fascination for the passing scenes.

They watched two men load a fridge on to a barge already groaning with electrical equipment. Their waterbus chugged on, foaming at the prow, zig-zagging from one side of the great canal to the other. Suzy drew Fiorenzo's attention to the eight or so commuters standing two-deep in the gondola which had operated as a ferry across the Grand Canal for centuries.

Fiorenzo didn't speak, his keen eyes observing everything greedily. The skyline of domes and leaning belltowers. The incomparable terraces of ancient palaces on either side of the canal, jostling for room. Rotting watergates and decayed jetties, striped, coroneted poles. A smart, highly varnished launch bearing demure little girls with their party dresses frothing in pink frills beneath warm coats and eyes huge with excitement. Venetians on the water-bus reading newspapers, quite accustomed to a daily journey through a city built on water and awash in history.

It seemed he devoured the sights with an almost desperate yearning, as if he'd longed to be there for years. He seethed with a passion that—try as he might to hide it—shone from his eyes like a beacon, betraying the fact that he felt a powerful emotion about Venice.

Suzy understood its pull. She never tired of it. No other high street like this one in the world. No other city so untouched by war, or so beautiful in all the changing seasons and the extraordinary quality of the light which had attracted painters for centuries.

She became aware that Fiorenzo had leaned forwards in his seat, his arm lightly resting on her shoulder. His eyes were as soft as black velvet, absorbed by a Venetian father on a landing stage unashamedly kissing his son's face with an exuberance that was making the little boy squeal in delight. Suzy's own mouth curved into a wistful smile at the happy child. He was dark and plump with rosy cheeks and bundled up against the cold, his long black lashes quite heart-stopping.

But it was the look on Fiorenzo's face which made Suzy's heart lurch and flutter with an erratic beat. He was touched by the child, and Fiorenzo's autocratic face with its habitually bleak expression had become gentle and loving. Oh, yes, she thought. He might have been brought up in England, but he was Italian through and through. For didn't every Mafia hood adore his mother and his children?

'Isn't he sweet?' she enthused, hoping to get on the right side of him. 'Italians really love their children, don't they?'

'Some do, some don't.'

Winter had returned to his face. 'I've never seen an Italian mistreat a child in all the years I've been in Italy,' she asserted wistfully, thinking how much Mario would have loved a son. And so would she.

'Stick around. Prepare to have your eyes opened,' he said grimly. 'Been here long?'

'Four years.'

'You don't miss England?'

'I *was* going home,' she confessed. 'Mario, my husband, had thrown me out——'

'Why?'

She gave a quick frown. 'Personal reasons,' she muttered. She wasn't going to tell this cynical man that she couldn't produce living sons. 'Anyway, I had to save more money for the air ticket. I'd seen a job advertised here, in Venice. I blew my savings on the rail fare and landed the job. Once here, I forgot about going back to England.'

'I envy you.' Fiorenzo's face harrowed, he watched as a laconic waterman, one foot on the tiller of a cement barge, suddenly opened his mouth and launched into a full-throated passionate aria, his voice quavering with the wake of the water-bus. The stately, silent progress of a passing gondola was disturbed by the wake, too, endangering the safety of a chipped stone angel propped up in the gondola's black-fringed seat. Fiorenzo heaved a deep sigh. 'I've missed all this. To think I could have lived here all my life...'

'Good heavens! A convert already! And you've only been here for three days!' she laughed.

He turned his slow, calculating gaze on her. 'How did you know that?' he murmured, a malevolent gleam in his eyes. 'Have you been following me or something, Suzy?' he scolded mockingly, his hand closing over her shoulder in a relentless grip.

She went cold to her bones. 'You told me,' she bluffed. 'Last night, when you were dazed. Oh, look,' she cried hastily, patting his knee excitedly and giving him a brilliant, eager smile. 'Look back down the canal a bit. I forgot to point out Desdemona's house—you know, like in *Othello*. And that's the Gritti Palace——'

'And this one, coming up on our right?' he asked silkily. 'With the wooden structure on the roof?'

Suzy's nerves were shot to pieces. She was sure he knew the building. He was pretending not to. And he also knew that she had tailed him. The only question was, what would he do about it? She leaned against the window to escape his intimidating body, and he crushed her there, apparently eager to look out. She bit her lip hard, frightened. He'd throw her in the canal if it suited him.

'The wooden platform? It's an *altana*,' she said in a slightly croaky voice. 'In the Middle Ages the women would sit there on the roof and bleach their hair a Titian gold——'

'No,' he said gently, neatly injecting a thread of steel into the word. 'The building beneath it, with those green-striped poles and the small jetty. Is it a palace?' he asked with deceptive innocence.

She licked her lips. 'Most of them are,' she said in an offhand tone. 'Um ... that's the Palazzo Moroschini.'

His brooding eyes devoured the façade. Suzy shivered at the raw emotion in his face as he took in every detail of the gorgeous Renaissance building with its white stucco, the small stone balconies, the massive watergate which had once received the treasures of the East.

He was utterly still beside her, but she could feel the blistering hatred in him, pouring out at the inoffensive *palazzo*. She feared that he was planning some way of gaining entrance, so that he could confront the Contessa with his blackmailing demands.

The little water-bus ploughed on, heading for the Accademia stop. He had eyes only for the *palazzo*. And, when Suzy flickered a nervous sideways glance at him, she was startled to see that there was something about his expression that was infinitely sad.

Her insatiable curiosity burned to be satisfied. She would find out what had caused this hatred between Fiorenzo and the Contessa. She'd always been able to clarify situations. It was becoming her trademark.

Her tact had served her well. In Naples, when she was first married, she had worked for an insurance investigator in the filing department. Dropping delicate hints, she'd suggested ways and means of exposing fraud, and the investigator had gratefully written her a glowing reference for her new job in Venice.

Maybe she could soften Fiorenzo's heart. Her hopes rose. 'There's a contessa living there,' she ventured. 'And a Prince Moroschini.'

His jaw clenched. 'Prince?' he repeated softly.

'That's not as grand as it sounds. Venetian princelings are ten a penny,' she said casually. 'His name is Guido.

He's the Contessa's son. Guido's very friendly—quite ordinary, really.'

'Ordinary, you say. Is that so?'

Fiorenzo looked quite fascinated. At least the heat was off her for the moment. 'I've met him once or twice at dinners where I've been working,' she said, thinking that it was true, she *had* done so—as part of the security arrangements. 'He's awfully nice. You'd never know he was a prince, to look at him.'

'Fancy that. Tell me about the family,' he said tensely.

'Oh, you want the gossip!' she laughed. 'Tabloid stuff. "Prince Dies in Tragic Accident".' Her face became serious. 'That was the last prince, of course, the twin brother of the Contessa. It only happened four months ago,' she said, hoping to provoke another reaction. But Fiorenzo's face had become shuttered. 'There was some sort of accident at their villa on the island they own, out there in the lagoon.'

'What accident?' he snapped.

'I don't know. The Contessa was involved——'

'I bet.'

Suzy shot him a puzzled glance. 'She was so badly injured that she ended up in a wheelchair.'

Fiorenzo's breath rasped out. 'A *wheelchair*?'

Suzy was startled. It seemed that he hadn't known that. Maybe he'd reconsider his blackmail now. Eagerly she decided to fill in more details and appeal to whatever sense of decency he might have.

'She's a tragic figure—awfully brave. She can't walk. Isn't that sad? Guido is a private doctor, and treats her. He's devoted to her. They're a devoted family, in fact. The old prince was a bit mad, so the rumour goes. He hadn't been seen in public for years and years. The story is that the Contessa half killed herself looking after him, refusing to let anyone else take care of him but herself and Guido. It's rather touching,' she mused.

'Very. Family affection; nothing more powerful.'

Tense-jawed, Fiorenzo stared out of the window, but Suzy knew from his distant expression that he saw nothing of the buildings which they passed. His eyes closed in a sudden pain which he couldn't control.

'What is it?' she asked gently. 'You're upset about something.'

'Upset? Me? What have I got to be upset about? We're coming up to the Rialto Bridge,' he said abruptly. 'Isn't this where you want to get out?'

Disappointed, Suzy fell silent. At the market she shopped carefully, unnerved by Fiorenzo's hard-eyed scrutiny. She was determined to prove to him that she was buying food for a luncheon. She moved about the laden fish-stalls in the fish market, looking as capable and experienced as possible, choosing spider crab and red mullet, then filled a bag with sweet potatoes from a canopied barge moored in a canal. Her money was running out. She had enough for some beans and perhaps a few artichokes.

'Is that all?' he asked, when she told him she'd finished.

'The other food is already there,' she lied unhappily. 'It's not a very big dinner.'

'It can't be. And what about all your equipment?' he murmured. 'Is that there too? I noticed you had no commercial catering stuff at your flat.'

'Heavens, no! I have a room in the building with everything I need in it,' she said, cold inside at his questioning. 'You needn't come any further. Go off and explore. See a few churches. I'm sure you haven't seen San Giacometto,' she said waspishly. It must be the only church in Venice he hadn't. 'I'm only going to the next street. Thanks and——'

He stopped her from taking the bags from him. 'I'll see you to the door.'

'Oh. How kind.' Down the street she came to what she hoped looked like a confident halt in front of a likely-looking house, and he dumped the bags by the door. To her alarm, he read the names of the people in the flats. 'Doesn't look smart, does it? But you should see inside!' she enthused.

'So this is where you're cooking a meal?'

'I wash up, too, don't forget,' she said, elaborating, raising her eyes to heaven. It was all vaguely true, she supposed. She cooked, she washed up. 'Oh, those endless dishes!'

He smiled faintly. 'Can I give you a call? I have your number. I'll be in Venice for some time. And I do want to see you again.'

'Please,' she said warmly. 'Call soon.'

She badly wanted to divert him from his course of action. If she chatted to him about the Contessa, and explained to him how frustrated Flavia had become at not being able to walk any more, he might relent. Her hand lifted as if to ring the bell. He took her hand and kissed it, bending low like a courtier. Then, as Suzy looked down on his dark head and attentive face she saw his eyebrows draw together. Slowly, he turned her hand over and kissed the whole of her soft palm with great concentration, and then dropped a light kiss on each of her long, elegantly manicured nails. When he lifted his head she saw a glitter in his eyes that was a little disconcerting.

'You'll be hearing from me,' he said softly. His finger touched her lips. When she opened her mouth to speak, he bent and kissed her, so that the faint rush of breath from his body flowed into her mouth, making her shudder. And then he strode away, pausing at the end of the street, watching her.

She waved, managed a smile, and rang the bell, picking up the bags, a faint unease in her mind. There was something nagging at her, something she knew about but couldn't put her finger on. The door opened and, seeing that he'd disappeared, Suzy began to make her excuses, and wished she could settle the sense of foreboding inside her.

CHAPTER FOUR

FURIOUS to her fingertips that she'd got herself into a web of deceit, Suzy stomped home with her crab and mullet and vegetables. She trudged up the stairs to her flat, and then doggedly plodded all the way back through the city. Weaving her way through a sea of grey pigeons and even greyer-looking tourists in St Mark's square, she headed for the Moroschini Palace.

She pulled on the Moor's-head bell and waited patiently by the high, ornamental iron gate, peering into the courtyard with its overgrown well-head, the plane tree and tangle of bare-stemmed, rambling roses. In a moment or two she saw the stocky figure of Alfonso, the family boatman, shuffling slowly over the flagstones. She gave a wry smile. Burly, surly and dejected as usual.

'Buongiorno. Come stai?' she enquired politely. One day she'd get a pleasant greeting out of him.

Not today. The thick-set Venetian shrugged, his face set in its usual attitude of sullen boredom, and he muttered something about being tired. Tired! He wasn't exactly over-stretched. Suzy didn't know why the Contessa kept him on. Guido said he'd been in the family ever since he could remember. It was a pretty generous loyalty to an old family retainer who could have been a stand-in for Grumpy—but that was the Contessa for you.

She followed the heavily built Alfonso across the yard and up the wide stone steps to the first-floor entrance. As she passed through the big hall which ran the whole length of the palace, she heard a strange thudding noise.

It was a sound she'd heard somewhere before, but couldn't place it...

Alfonso's pace suddenly accelerated. He positively drove Suzy up the barrel-vaulted staircase to the old business quarter, and this time, in answer to her questions, he muttered about renovations. Suzy was surprised. She had thought the Contessa was counting the pennies.

She waited in the dark gallery which served as an anteroom, wondering what all the battered suitcases were doing there. It looked as if the Moroschinis were going away.

The noise from below stopped. Suzy sat down on a lyre-backed couch covered in priceless Fortuny fabric, and passed the time by playing princess. These family paintings were her ancestors, the bronzes of Venetian lions and eagles were hers, the dusty chandeliers, too. And if she were a princess here, she'd have a moan at the contract cleaners who were supposed to keep the palace in order. The place was filthy.

Glad to have a break from what seemed like endless walking, Suzy stretched her aching legs out on the threadbare Persian rug and dreamed for several minutes, wondering what it would be like to live in a real Renaissance palace. Then she grinned. Princess Suzy just didn't sound right. She'd stick with Suzy the Sleuth.

'Suzy! Lovely to see you.'

She turned and smiled at Guido—Prince Moroschini; his sturdy figure never managing to look princely, no matter how expensive his clothes were. He could have been a commoner, not a prince whose ancestors went back to the twelfth century. His mother was different, however. Put the Contessa in sackcloth, and the blue blood would glow through the hessian.

'Hello, Guido. Are you going away? You haven't been frightened off by Fiorenzo Veronese, have you?' she asked.

'Good lord, no!' grinned Guido. 'Far from it. Mother's in very good spirits. We've managed to let the *palazzo* to a wealthy American banker through his Venetian agent. He wants it to entertain business clients, apparently. Short notice—he's coming this afternoon, having discovered that it's Carnival time. Still, what do you do when a man writes enough noughts on the cheque to clear the national debt?'

Suzy laughed. 'I'm glad. Where will you stay? Your villa on the lagoon?'

Guido's face darkened. 'No. We haven't been there since my uncle died. I suppose it'll go to rack and ruin eventually. So we're off to our villa in Asolo.'

'It'll give you both a break and take your minds off Fiorenzo Veronese. Do you want me to carry on tailing him?'

Guido smiled, looking very self-satisfied. 'I don't think there's anything more you can do,' he said. Suzy didn't know whether to be relieved or disappointed.

'My dear! You've come! Have some bubbly!'

Suzy jumped up as the beautifully groomed Contessa Flavia glided in silently, her electric wheelchair making hardly any sound. 'Good morning, Contessa,' she smiled. 'You look marvellous.' Flavia was positively glowing, her skin flushed, her eyes bright as if she was filled to the brim with joy.

'I feel wonderful! Put it down there, 'Fonso,' said Flavia to Alfonso, who had followed the azure-blue-gowned Contessa with a tray bearing champagne and crystal glasses. Suzy thought that the Contessa had been celebrating for some time, judging by the way her hand was shaking, and the sparkle in her eyes rivalled the champagne itself.

The Titian-haired Flavia lifted her fizzling glass. '*Salute!*' she cried exuberantly. 'To a golden future. One without any cares in the world.'

'I'll drink to that,' said Suzy fervently. 'Contessa . . . I don't want to cast a blight on your happiness, but I think I'd better warn you that Fiorenzo Veronese is almost definitely going to cause trouble. I'm a little worried that you're intending to go away——'

The older woman smiled contentedly. 'I don't think we have anything to worry about.' She exchanged glances with Alfonso, who shrugged and shambled out.

Suzy was puzzled. 'Has there been a new development? Have you seen him today and persuaded him to stop persecuting you?'

'Not exactly. Since it was your day off yesterday, we sent 'Fonso to watch his apartment,' said Guido cheerfully. 'Veronese never slept there last night. Mother thinks he's given up—probably gone home.'

'Oh! I'm afraid that's not the reason he didn't go back to his apartment. You see, I didn't take the day off,' said Suzy. 'I wanted to stay on his track. Last night I saw him—and he saw me. I had to blow my cover.' She watched with surprise as the liquid in the Contessa's crystal goblet slopped on to the table.

'You . . . followed him?' Flavia mopped up the mess with a lace handkerchief. 'Last night? But I *insisted* you had a rest.'

'I know, it was sweet of you, and so thoughtful to think I might need a day off. But I wanted to help you. I was actually going home when it happened.'

The Contessa's hands gripped the arms of the wheelchair. 'When *what* happened?' she demanded sharply.

Suzy briefly outlined the events of the evening. When she began to explain about the police launch, Flavia sat erect and listened intently with an increasing agitation.

'My God! He—he wasn't...*hurt?*' breathed the Contessa.

That was typical of her, thought Suzy. Her worst enemy, and she's concerned about him. 'Shaken, that's all,' she said reassuringly.

There was a long silence. The Contessa set her chair in motion, powering herself up and down the long room so vigorously that the suspended marble floor trembled on its wooden beams. Guido was staring out of the window, his shoulders tensed up as if he'd forgotten to breathe. The glass goblet dropped to the floor from his nerveless fingers and shattered into smithereens.

'*Madonna!* He's there!' he whispered. He let rip another oath, an earthier one this time. 'He has come!'

'Veronese?' Suzy strode angrily over to the window. It was too high for the Contessa to see out, and Flavia sat helplessly in her chair, her whole body straining, her neck arched up as she tried to see over the ledge.

The snow was falling again, its mantle of white turning Venice into an elaborately iced wedding-cake. Across the Grand Canal there was a tiny square, a *campo*, which ran down to the water's edge. And it was here that Fiorenzo stood, staring up at the palace, a dark, motionless figure.

Snow fell unheeded on his bared head. He stood as still as a statue carved from ivory and ebony, glowering at the palace as if nothing else existed for him in the whole wide world. His eyes were fixed to the coat of arms above the watergate, which admonished the Moroschini heirs to 'secure the bloodline, pure and true.' As he read the Latin inscription, he appeared to become taller, more arrogant, more menacing than ever.

'He's got a nerve!' said Suzy, aware of Flavia's laboured breathing behind her. 'Talk about bare-faced cheek!'

'What's he doing? Is he coming over, across the *canale*? What does he look like?' cried Flavia hoarsely.

Like a prince, Suzy wanted to say. A haughty aristocrat, with a supreme confidence radiating from him. Proud. She wisely kept silent.

'Determined, hostile and utterly ruthless,' muttered Guido. 'Like a bloody vulture watching his prey... How dare he? To come almost to our door——'

'Dear God! What does he mean to do?' cried Flavia, clutching at Guido's jacket. She raised her elegantly coiffed head. 'To come so close... Will he talk to the neighbours? To the tradesmen? Stop him, Guido! Keep him away!' she cried incoherently.

Suzy stared at her in consternation. The Contessa looked petrified. All colour had drained from her face. Her mouth trembled and her eyes were quite hunted. This Fiorenzo was more of a threat than Suzy had imagined. What did he know? What was the guilty secret which the Contessa wouldn't divulge?

Guido caressed his mother's head. He looked just as alarmed. 'What are *we* going to do?' he asked in a strained voice. 'We agreed to the American coming only because we thought Veronese had left Venice! We can't leave the *palazzo* now. You said Alfonso was certain that the swine had gone, Mother. You said we had nothing to worry about.'

'He was certain. We both were,' whispered Flavia. 'Damn him! Damn him to eternity!' she grated, startling Suzy with her venom.

'I think you ought to tell me what's going on,' said Suzy quietly. 'If I'm to help you——'

'Yes, yes. In a minute,' cut in Flavia irritably. 'Oh, forgive me, Suzy, for being a sharp old woman, but I feel so helpless! My legs...' She smiled weakly at Suzy's gesture of sympathy. 'I must think. He's ruined my plans.

We definitely can't go back on the deal with the American. It's for three months! Oh, damn Fiorenzo!'

Flavia's big brown eyes filled with tears. Suzy impulsively crouched beside her, resting a sympathetic hand on the rug-covered knees, unable to bear seeing the unfortunate woman so desperately unhappy. The last few months must have been hell on earth for her. She'd lost a twin brother, and had been paralysed. Now Fiorenzo was threatening her good name.

'We'll think of something between us,' soothed Suzy. 'If you'd only tell me——'

Guido abandoned the window abruptly. 'He's gone,' he said, taking his mother's hands in his. 'Gone, Mother. Vanished into the snow.'

'I'd like to make him vanish!' muttered Flavia. 'If I wasn't a prisoner of this wretched chair, I'd tackle Veronese myself. If I was a whole woman again...' Her voice trailed away miserably and ended in a shuddering sob.

'What is he threatening you with?' persisted Suzy.

'Scandal,' said Flavia bitterly. 'It would rock Venice. Ruin us. He demands this palace as the price for his silence. How can I give it up? I've lived here all my life! That cold, callous man wants to strut about in my home——'

'The palace? That's ludicrous! Surely whatever he threatens can't be worth that! Fight him,' said Suzy grimly, wishing the Contessa would confide in her. 'Tell him to go to hell. Denounce him to the police.'

'I can't,' whispered Flavia brokenly. 'You English don't understand honour. The disgrace... If it came out... I'd rather live in poverty than surrender my good name! What friends would I have? A poor Contessa is still a Contessa. A dishonoured one is nothing.'

The distraught Flavia clung to Suzy with such a powerful grip that she winced. For a frail, pain-racked invalid, Flavia was in astonishingly good shape. 'Can't I do something? I want to help. You've been so good to me,' said Suzy soberly, determined to get the better of the evil Veronese.

'We need the American's money. But we can't stay here with him. Yet someone must be around to stop Fiorenzo gaining access to the palace. Once in, he'd never leave,' said Flavia.

'We must use delaying tactics,' decided Guido. 'Tell him we have urgent business in Asolo. 'Fonso can drop a letter in his door hinting that we'll definitely come to an agreement on our return.'

Flavia brightened. 'Good! Suzy, you must stay in the palace to keep an eye on things for us. I've hired a maid and housekeeper as I usually do, why shouldn't there be...say...an interpreter?' Flavia began to look excited as her plans began to unravel in her mind. 'My dear, you'll do it, won't you? Report to us each night. Fiorenzo must not set foot in this house!'

Suzy hesitated. Flavia's pleading eyes, her evident dependence persuaded her. 'I'll keep him out,' she promised.

'Could she go with 'Fonso to pick Mr Verreaux up at the Excelsior this afternoon?' suggested Guido. 'When we've welcomed the man we can leave.'

'Yes. We mustn't stay around. Not now,' muttered Flavia.

'I won't let you down,' said Suzy quietly.

Flavia gave a radiant smile. 'You're a good girl. When my brother's money comes through, I'll give you a bonus.'

'Thank you. Though...you won't forget the down payment we agreed on, will you?' reminded Suzy awkwardly. She had been waiting to broach the subject. Flavia had forgotten to leave the cheque she had promised.

'Of course! We have money from Verreaux,' beamed
Flavia, motioning for Guido to pay her. 'There's one
more thing you can do for me——' The Contessa broke
off and turned to Guido again. 'Darling, you run off
and see your friends in Florian's. I have a couple of
things to arrange with Suzy about bedrooms and so on.
I thought the attic room for her? Mr Verreaux might
want to have guests to stay overnight, so we must leave
the others free.'

Guido nodded. When he had left, the Contessa leaned
back in her chair looking utterly devastated, and Suzy's
heart went out to her. 'You've had a hard time,
Contessa.'

'It's been one thing after another,' Flavia said weakly.
'You won't let Fiorenzo in, will you? He'll try to steal
family papers, hoping to prove his outrageous claims.'

'If they're outrageous, then why be afraid of them?'
asked Suzy uncertainly.

'Because he's so convincing!'

'It's all lies, then?'

'Of course! But here they listen to gossip, and it
grows... He's threatening to expose an——' She plucked
at her blanket. 'I can't say it,' she breathed. 'It's better
you don't know the filth he's invented. It concerns
Guido, and I must protect him. He's my son! He's more
important to me than anything in the world. I've devoted my whole life, my energies, my ambitions to him.
Please understand?'

Suzy clasped her hand and nodded, reluctantly ac-
cepting that her curiosity would have to remain unsat-
isfied. 'I do. I'm sorry,' she said gently. 'If I had a child,
I'd do anything for him, too.'

'You never had children? I'm surprised,' said the
Contessa, her eyes eagle-hard, prompting an explanation.

Suzy bit her lip. 'I miscarried twice,' she explained
quietly. 'I was told I'd never carry a child full-term.' She

thought of the anguish and the distress when she had discovered Mario had a pregnant mistress waiting to step into her shoes.

'Poor girl! Never to be a mother. How hard it will be for you to remarry—certainly in this country. I must tell Guido. When he marries you can come to our palace often and share his children,' said Flavia, looking suddenly cheerful again. 'Go and pack, my dear. Look after my palace for me, keep a weather-eye open for that degenerate. And whatever you do, remember—don't believe a word Fiorenzo tells you. He was born a liar. He lies with his lips, his voice, his eyes and, most of all, he lies with his heart.'

Suzy had found Flavia's sympathy a double-edged sword. She knew already that few men—particularly in this country—would consider marrying her, knowing she couldn't give them sons. Flavia was offering her what amounted to a second home. Strange, though, that the Contessa hadn't remembered that she'd have to give up the palace if she was to stop Fiorenzo from spreading rumours.

It was almost as if Flavia was certain Fiorenzo would never succeed. She smiled. She wouldn't put it past the woman to have a crafty plan. She certainly had a quick mind.

On her way home she walked past Harry's Bar, her collar turned up against the bitter blizzard, and came across Guido, chatting with some of his friends. He slipped away from them and hurried up to her.

'Come and have a coffee with me,' he said eagerly. 'I won't see you for a while and there's something I want to tell you.'

'About Veronese?' she asked.

He frowned. 'Oh. Yes, well, I could do that, too. Coming?'

Guido gallantly protected her from the worst of the snowstorm by tucking an arm around her shoulder. They turned their backs to the weather and made for the eighteenth-century café beneath the arcades in the Piazza San Marco.

Florian's was crowded. The café consisted of a series of narrow rooms, each only large enough to hold a dozen or so, and everyone who was anyone wanted to be in there, in Lavena's, or in Quadri's across the square. Guido looked around irritably and caught a waiter's eye while Suzy rubber-necked at the period furnishings and the romantic Oriental figures painted on the mirrored walls. It was wonderfully decadent, smelling of rich Arabic coffee, hot pastries and tangy aftershave.

'You're so enthusiastic about everything,' smiled Guido, looking at her dancing eyes. His arm rested on her shoulder. 'I get on better with you than any woman I've known. You really love Venice, don't you?'

'Yes, enormously,' she grinned, giving him an affectionate, friendly hug. 'And I'm going to do everything I can to stop that awful man from hurting you and your mother.'

An American couple dressed as Harlequins vacated their seats, intimidated by the hovering waiter. She and Guido surrendered their coats to the waiter and sat on the banquette. Guido slipped some money into the waiter's hand, then ordered coffee and cakes.

Suzy smiled ruefully. Guido had said he was broke. Poverty was relative; the waiter had just been tipped sufficient *lire* to feed her for a week—and coffee here alone cost as much as a simple snack-bar meal at a counter. Appearances were everything for men like Guido.

She sat beneath a mirror bearing a figure of a nine-teenth-century Arab, breathing in the aromas, listening to the buzz of conversation, seeing the extravagant gestures, smiling at the theatrical cries as people recognised one another. It was her first and last time here, and she wanted to imprint it on her mind. Her eyes strayed around the elegant women, the immaculately turned-out men, refined and imperious. She smiled at Guido. He did look out of place—bluff, hearty, solid.

'Suzy,' he murmured affectionately.

'Tell me about Fiorenzo,' she said.

'Oh. All right. Quietly,' he warned, drawing her nearer on the plum-coloured velvet, so that she was squashed against his hip. 'We don't want anyone to hear us discussing him.'

'I want to know who he is,' she insisted. 'And what he's done.'

'That's easy,' he said grimly. 'He's a ruthless swine. He made his father's life a living hell. God, you should have seen his tantrums! He'd scream the house down, almost every day.'

'He lived with you?' The astounded Suzy wondered if Fiorenzo was the son of a servant.

'He did—for the first few years of his life. His mother died, so my mother brought Fiorenzo up. We're the same sort of age. He was always getting into scrapes, having accidents, being disobedient. It was like having a wild animal in the house. Mother stuck it out till he was seven, but by then she was at the end of her tether.' He paused, waiting while the waiter laid down a tray in front of them.

'He's some sort of a distant relation, then?' asked Suzy, fascinated. She sipped her iced water and chose a chocolate *tartufo*, trying to visualise a younger, totally uninhibited version of the guarded but savage Fiorenzo.

'Distant's the word! He shut himself off from everyone. Once or twice he'd come back for a visit with the woman we paid to look after him in Switzerland. God knows why. He wouldn't even speak to any of us, least of all his father.'

'He did have a father, then?'

'Oh, yes. Fiorenzo is a cousin of mine.' Guido stared glumly at the tiny marble table. 'He disappeared off the face of the earth six years ago, and we were all heartily glad. To be honest, we thought he must be dead. Anyway, Mother and I breathed a sigh of relief when he went. So did his father.'

'His father? His very own father?' Her mind mulled over the unusual family split. Italians might flout every law in the book, but family life was sacrosanct. She was appalled. And she realised that this fitted with what Fiorenzo had told her—that his father had been 'dead' as far as he was concerned. 'Guido, why did his father hate him?'

'He's a cold-hearted, vindictive little bastard, that's why,' muttered Guido savagely.

'Well, well. I think you must be talking about me.'

The effect of Fiorenzo's softly menacing voice was electric. Guido's coffee splashed on the table as he whirled around. Suzy jerked back automatically, pressing herself into Guido's shoulder to avoid the hot liquid.

'Get out of here!' seethed Guido, mopping his fingers with a shaking hand. 'How dare you eavesdrop?'

Fiorenzo leaned his black-coated bulk on the small, circular table, his big hands planted on either side as if he might take a fancy to ripping it out of the floor. His slow gaze surveyed Suzy's closeness to Guido, and an unpleasant sneer pulled down the corners of his mouth.

'Oh, very cosy. Cuddles in the café,' he mocked.

'What a dirty mind you have! We were having a civilised coffee before you turned up,' said Suzy sharply, glaring at him from under her lashes.

Guido seemed incapable of speech, and she could feel his knee quivering beside hers. She shifted her leg to help steady him and show him that she was with him the whole of the way. Fiorenzo's eyes narrowed to pinpoints of contempt, flickering cold scorn at her.

'So you *are* part of the Moroschini menagerie, after all, part of that den of iniquity? And you *were* following me, weren't you?' he said, with an icy frown.

'You ungrateful man! If you're talking about last night when I got you out of the canal, I was going home,' she snapped.

'From what?'

She drew in an exasperated breath, which she let out rapidly when she saw Fiorenzo's eyes cynically observing the rapid rise of her soft breasts beneath the wool dress.

'Diverting,' he murmured. 'But not diverting enough. From *what*?' The words were hurled at her with the force of a hammer-throw. Fiorenzo was angry beneath that poker-face.

'Produce your Interpol card and I'll tell you,' she said coldly. 'Otherwise you can take a running jump. I don't have to answer your impertinent questions. If I'd known what kind of man you are, I'd have left you to sink in the mud,' she added sourly.

'And I wouldn't have been warned about that police launch in time and I would have died,' he said softly. 'Interfering little bitch, isn't she, Guido?' he remarked, switching his steady black glare to the prince.

Guido's hand shook with anger, and Suzy touched it sympathetically. The gesture was not lost on Fiorenzo.

'Sweet. Very touching. So you're a cook, eh? Cooking up what?' he asked sarcastically. 'Bedtime snacks? Nightcaps, delivered to Guido's room? Well, I suppose it's only to be expected. You're just up Guido's street. He always preferred servant girls to the daughters of the nobility. God knows, his mother's tried to marry him off enough times to suitable women of breeding. Flavia must be really worried about the prospect of you becoming her daughter-in-law. Don't be too hopeful. She'll find some reason to put Guido off you.'

'Keep out of my affairs!' said Guido nervously.

'You're out of order, Veronese!' cried Suzy hotly, flushing a deep pink with embarrassment.

'I have an interest in you. I feel a certain possessiveness towards you. I slept in your bed, after all,' he drawled, his eyes carnal with the memory. The smooth skin on his face seemed to tauten over the bones, and make his eyes and mouth more compelling than ever. Sexual hunger flowed from him, enveloping her in its invigorating power.

'Shut up!' she seethed. Every inch of her body was tingling. She touched her breast as if to calm her thudding heart, so he wouldn't see the way it pounded, but his eyes were already there, avid and greedy as if he was imagining placing his lips to each nipple... She squirmed, and he laughed gently, knowing she was unwillingly aroused. Her eyes flew up to rage silently at him.

'You insolent devil!' breathed Guido.

Fiorenzo gave Suzy a mocking, knowing stare. 'It's true,' he murmured in an amused tone. 'We even shared her bed for a tumble or two. And I kissed her till she couldn't breathe. Nice mouth.' He licked his lips salaciously, and Suzy clenched her teeth together to prevent herself from copying the action. 'And incredible——'

'You swine!' spat Guido. 'How dared you touch her?'

'Jealous?' enquired Fiorenzo, his eyes glittering. 'I must tell your mother. Or is she hoping your affair will die a death when you've had what you want?'

'You are no gentleman!' ground Guido.

'My dear cousin! Neither are you,' said Fiorenzo calmly. 'At least my behaviour is only due to lack of upbringing, not birth.'

Guido's body became stiff with frustrated rage. The two men faced each other like warring dogs, although one was controlled and contemptuous, sure of his ground and confident of victory.

'I don't know what the hell you mean! You out-and-out bastard!' whispered Guido, white-lipped, his voice croaking. 'Insult me if you must, but you've got no right to embarrass Suzy and broadcast whatever depravity you forced on her——'

'Hasn't she told you what we did in her flat?' Fiorenzo's eyebrow raised lazily in astonishment. 'Such fun. About how we played doctors and nurses... Of course, that was after she stripped my wet clothes off. Such a delicate hand on one's zip.'

'That's *enough*!' gritted Suzy, her eyes lashing his like the blades of a sword. She was on fire, burning from inside with an almost unquenchable anger. This man had gone beyond the bounds of normal human behaviour, taunting her, tormenting Guido, taking a consummate pleasure in plunging the knife in both of them. It was despicable to speak of something private that had happened between them. 'Now I know what the Contessa meant when she said you could turn rumour into truth! You'd twist anything to make it fit your evil mind! What a thoroughly offensive, diabolically depraved man you are!'

'Yes. And don't you forget that,' snarled Fiorenzo, his anger leaping to the surface, matching hers in a brief, sparking flash of heat. Hostility surged across the table, hitting Suzy like a blast from a furnace. Beneath all that ice he was pure, molten fury, she thought in alarm. 'Never underestimate my lack of normal emotion. It was killed off years ago. I learned to do without tenderness.' He gave a cold laugh. 'I was taught by an expert.'

'Leave her alone!' muttered Guido resentfully. 'And keep your voice down, for God's sake!'

Fiorenzo ignored Guido, his glittering eyes still slicing into Suzy. 'Whatever your job really is,' he grated through his teeth, 'and whatever you're thinking of doing, I warn you; get in my way, and you'll get hurt. It's a simple case of cause and effect.'

'I don't know what you're talking about,' she said coldly. 'Prince Moroschini——'

'Who?' asked Fiorenzo in a deceptively soft voice.

Suzy eyed him haughtily. She indicated the red-faced Guido. 'Guido. Prince Moro——'

'Oh, yes. I forgot. The doctor himself. What did you do, buy yourself the qualification? I can't imagine you passed the exams, *Prince* Moroschini...' Fiorenzo's voice trailed away, his features showing a sudden blind fury. 'You arrogant son-of-a-bitch!' he snarled, shock waves of temper shaking every tensed muscle, and Suzy felt the solid little table tremble beneath his hands. Fiorenzo's black, fathomless eyes studied Guido's frightened face as if they were making a silent vow. Then he straightened, an immense dignity about his dark figure.

'Fiorenzo! I beg you! Accept the situation——'

He cut Guido off with a dismissive wave of an imperious hand. 'I never have, I never will, Principe. Oh, the awesome power of a title!' he said scornfully, making a valiant attempt to control himself. 'It gets you the best seats—yes, I saw the by-play with those Americans that your name and casually tossed money created—it gets you easy credit, respect, a packed social life. How you love it all! The admiration, the conquests you can make of shop-girls, waitresses——'

'Shut up!' seethed Guido, going white.

'The playboy prince,' said Fiorenzo scornfully. 'With all that a title can bring. And, if I don't interfere, the probate will be filed soon and you'll have the Moroschini wealth too. I can understand why Flavia wrote telling me to go to hell,' he growled.

'It's where unwanted, unloved bastards like you belong!' grated Guido.

Suzy felt Fiorenzo's violent flinch echo through her own body. All anger drained from his face, leaving it haggard and desolate. She was terribly upset by what was happening. This wasn't the talk of cousins, not in a family-based society like Italy's. Relations might quarrel, argue with violent emotions, all guns blazing, but their anger blew over and they stuck together through thick and thin. This was something different, and the undercurrents running through the bad feeling between Guido and Fiorenzo were very disturbing and sinister.

'You used to idolise me when we were boys together, Guido,' he said in an emotionless monotone, controlling himself with a supreme effort. 'You'd follow me around like a little dog. Remember how annoyed your mother was?'

'I was fooled by your bravado. You were a daredevil. She knew what you were like! She was protecting me!'

'She knew what she was creating,' corrected Fiorenzo in a quiet growl. 'A boy without a heart. Don't I recall tears from you, when I left?'

Guido flushed. 'That was years ago! We were seven-year-old kids. I thought you were fearless and exciting, reckless, even. It was before——'

'Before your vicious, malevolent and grasping mother poisoned your mind,' said Fiorenzo coldly. 'I wonder if there's any Borgia blood in the family?' he mused.

Suzy felt Guido tense. Outraged, she turned blazing eyes on Fiorenzo, her lip curled over bared teeth as if she wanted to bite him hard.

'You ill-mannered rat! To speak like that of a helpless woman! I'll stand witness if Prince Moroschini wants to sue you for slander!' she cried vehemently, aware that everyone in the room was listening with fascination to the exchange.

She coloured up, but stood her ground, even though her bristling figure seemed to afford Fiorenzo some faint amusement. She could feel Guido's knee trembling beside hers again. He was out of his depth, intimidated by his relentlessly taunting cousin.

'For God's sake, Fiorenzo!' groaned Guido. 'You're creating a public spectacle of yourself! We can't conduct this conversation——'

'I'll not be silenced. I came to warn you,' said Fiorenzo quietly to Suzy, a sinister threat giving a steel edge to his words. 'Keep out of this family affair. It's none of your business. It'll get nasty.' His mouth lifted at the corner in a cynical smile. 'I'm not exactly renowned for compassion. The compassion fairy seems to have passed me by. People in my way tend to get mown down.'

'I don't know what chip you've got on your shoulder——' Suzy began.

'Chip? Lord! I could build a log cabin with my chips!' he retorted with a savage coldness.

'I'm working for the family, and I stand by them,' she said defiantly, finding her hand gripped by Guido's under the table.

Fiorenzo had noticed the movement. His eyebrow lifted haughtily. 'What kind of work? Night work?' he sneered.

She and Guido jumped up at the insult, but Fiorenzo gave a mirthless laugh, looking through his lashes at them both impassively, as if they were dirt beneath his feet. He flicked his teeth with his thumb, the ultimate Italian insult, which brought a huge, indrawn breath from the aghast Guido.

'I won't forget this,' glowered Suzy. 'No man slangs me off and gets away with it.'

'Oh, good. Pistols at dawn,' Fiorenzo said sarcastically. 'Or are you intending to join your employer in planning to stab me in the back? Because if you are, I'll be ready for you this time. Besides, I have nothing to lose and everything to gain. *Arrivederci.*' His eyes glowed. 'I'll see you soon. Very soon. I think you'll enjoy the drama that is about to unfold.'

He gave a mock bow and then strode out, shouldering his way like a tornado through the group of waiters who'd watched the scene with awe, not daring to interrupt.

Guido was shaking with suppressed fury. 'Oh, my God!' he groaned. 'The shame of it! Mother will be absolutely appalled! For scandal to touch us——'

'I'm going after him,' Suzy said grimly.

'No!'

Determined, she slipped from Guido's restraining grasp, wriggled around the crowded tables and into the arcades outside. Fiorenzo was striding angrily towards the *campanile*, his long legs driving him at a relentless pace. She flew after him, and he suddenly turned at her running steps, half crouching, as if ready to fend off an attack. Suzy skidded to a puzzled halt, and then tipped up her chin and walked towards his straightening figure with all the dignity she could summon up.

'What's the matter? Guido throw you out?' he sneered, his teeth looking as sharp and white as a shark's.

'Let's talk.' Suzy gazed at him unblinkingly.

'I've done all the talking I want to.'

'I have things to say and I'm determined to say them.'

'I don't trust you,' he growled. He turned his big black collar up, his eyes brooding on her.

'I'm not carrying a weapon,' she said scornfully. 'If you weren't so free with your hands, I'd let you frisk me. Oh, this is stupid! You're not afraid of me, are you? Look, all I want is for you to lay off the Contessa.'

He contemplated her for a second or two, his face as blank as a carnival mask. 'You are aware that you've just sealed your own fate, I suppose, by openly admitting you're in collusion with her?'

Suzy lifted her proud chin. 'God, you're terrifying!' she scathed. 'I'm not intimidated,' she said, determinedly blocking out his hard, bone-chilling expression. 'I am trying to defend a half paralysed woman against a *monster*——'

'Why? She's perfectly capable of looking after herself. Don't let those big brown eyes fool you. She can turn on the tears at will. She'll crawl over shards of glass for her beloved Guido. Besides, he can defend her himself.'

'I'm tougher than him.'

'That's true. But then, so is a dollop of ice-cream.'

'You——!'

Fiorenzo's long lashes fluttered heavily in derision. 'Oh, don't waste my time by defending your lover. I must say, I'm surprised at your choice. I would have thought you preferred real men.'

'Big, rough ones, who bully defenceless women?' she sneered.

His mouth curled at the corners. Suzy found herself watching it turn up, fraction by fraction, and she knew she was holding her breath. She was almost mesmerised by him, by the power that poured out of him... energy, vitality... Her tongue slid over her dry mouth, and his lips parted. Dead give-away, she realised, knowing that she had betrayed herself. A predatory hunger filled his face. And her pulses leapt to see it.

'Exciting, isn't it, what there is between us?' he murmured silkily. 'Carnal, primitive—and quite undesirable. But it's there and will never go away. There's only one way to escape from it. Total immersion or total abstention.'

Suzy couldn't tear her eyes away from the arching bow of his mouth. Its sensuality just held her unwillingly in its thrall. The tip of his tongue touched his teeth, and she felt a spurt of heat coil in her loins.

'I think that what you feel and what I feel are two different things,' she said haughtily, her voice a little shaky.

'No,' he said, the suppressed power in his body making her tremble. 'We feel the same. I have to admit that I don't want to feel anything for anyone, Suzy, let alone lust.' He shrugged helplessly. 'Sex chooses the damnedest moments. Why don't we get it over and done with?' he suggested softly.

Her mouth had gone quite dry at the thought of touching him, giving in to the thudding urgency of her body. Her reaction to him bewildered and worried her. He possessed a kind of animal magnetism that was so sexual that she could almost touch it. If she reached out... Suddenly realising what was happening to her, she dropped her head to stare at the ground, fighting a fevered battle with her body.

'If this were three hundred years ago,' she said resentfully, 'you'd be hanging between the pillars on the Doge's Palace. That's where they executed criminals...' She almost said, 'and seducers', but she didn't want to give him ideas. He had enough already. 'Fiorenzo,' she said, with an effort at controlling her anger with him. 'I want you to reconsider your blackmail of the Contessa.'

'I suppose it might be amusing to be persuaded. Come on.'

He turned on his heel and started to walk away. 'What?' She stood simply staring at him in astonishment.

He looked back over his shoulder. 'I'm damned if I'm talking to you here. It's freezing.' His black eyes gleamed with amusement. 'Or hadn't you noticed? Steamed up to boiling point, were you?'

'I was rather angry, yes,' she said coolly.

He grinned. 'I'm so glad. It's always sweeter to conquer a woman who starts off hostile and plays hard to get,' he murmured.

'I'm not only that, I'm totally unavailable,' she retorted frostily.

'Coward,' he taunted.

'I am *not* a coward!' she cried hotly.

'Then take the risk,' he husked, his long, slow look reducing her to a bag of shaking bones and flesh with hardly any will at all. 'Love it or hate it, we'll be lovers. I mean to make love to you so thoroughly that you'll never forget me, no matter how many men you encounter after me.'

'You are so arrogant!' she stormed. 'Doesn't it occur to you that I actually find you disgusting? All right. So you know I've been tailing you. I'm a private investigator and I'm fully aware of what you're doing to the Contessa, and I think you're beneath contempt. Make love with you? I'd rather make love with a worm!'

'My dear girl, you'll achieve that ambition if you give yourself to Guido,' he drawled.

Suzy took two quick steps forwards to hit him, and then he wasn't there any more. Her arm seemed to be pinioned behind her back, and that was where Fiorenzo was, drawing her towards his chest. She slipped her foot swiftly around his ankle and bent to pull him off balance. That didn't work, either. She was somehow half lying across his bent knee, face up, and he was smiling down on her in triumph, to the delight of a group of passing tourists dressed as vampires.

'Let me get up!' she seethed, her back arching over his thigh and away from his slowly approaching chest.

'Pleasure. Just don't try to hurl me over your shoulder. I think I'm better trained than you,' he said smugly.

'Let me *up*!' Her neck was knotting with the effort of holding her head up and keeping an eye on what he was doing.

'Merciless bastard, aren't I?' he said with brutal satisfaction. His eyes glittered coldly. 'You can have a go at persuading me to give up my revenge. But don't put any money on succeeding. We'll take a gondola. That way, it'll be private. But public enough for you to feel safe. My treat.' He gave a humourless smile. 'I think I can afford it. I'm expecting to come into a lot of money soon.'

Suzy stared and followed his arrogant figure, her eyes vitriolic at the way his big black shoulders swaggered. She'd keep her temper and persevere till he saw that hounding the Contessa had no future and was shameful. Not that he'd care what anyone thought of him. Public censure didn't bother him at all; he would have thrown cups at the walls in Florian's if he'd thought it would have furthered his cause.

She ground her teeth. A man without ethics, without any conventions, or compassion, was almost impossible to coerce. It was like trying to dent solid ice with a toothbrush. He was impervious to charm, anger, scorn.

He must have a weak link somewhere. The only straw she could grasp at was that he wanted her. And using that could prove to be lethal as far as she was concerned. Thank God they were going to talk in a gondola. Anywhere else and she'd find herself flat on her back being propositioned again.

Fiorenzo stopped by the Paglia bridge and took her elbow in an authoritative grip. 'In here.' Suzy checked over the waiting gondola, which looked harmless enough. 'No leg-irons,' said Fiorenzo, amused by her hesitation. 'There's been a run on them lately.'

She made the mistake of haughtily tossing her head and stepping into the gondola, her suspicions quelled by his ridiculous remark. The moment she was in the boat, however, he put his hands under her armpits and lifted her bodily into the one moored alongside.

'What——?'

'Andiamo!' he snapped at the waiting gondolier.

Let's go? Fuming, with her legs dangling helplessly in mid-air, Suzy realised Fiorenzo had seized his opportunity to get her alone. For this gondola had a *felze*, a little cabin, where passers-by wouldn't see what he was doing to her. With the boat rocking dangerously, he bundled her into the plushly upholstered cabin, where he gently lowered her feet to the thick crimson carpet.

CHAPTER FIVE

THE curtain tassels began to swing gently. To Suzy's dismay, she saw that the gondolier had cast off and was poling the boat down the canal. Suzy held down her anger. He'd love a battle royal. So she'd freeze him out and hurt his vanity. If that didn't work, she'd crack those perfect teeth. They were probably caps, anyway.

'Do you honestly imagine that you can come on strong in one of these?' she asked coolly, staring around the claustrophobic little cabin.

'I could come on strong, as you put it, almost anywhere if you were around,' he said with a mocking smile. 'You arouse me very quickly. Not afraid of that? No? I do admire your composure. I dislike women who cry when I frighten them.'

She let her eyes show her contempt. 'Bully.'

'Very much so. I enjoy bringing women to their knees,' he said with a masculine, suggestive smirk. Suzy flushed at the sexual innuendo. 'When you beg for mercy—or for my favours—it'll be very satisfying.'

'More than that. It'll be a miracle,' she snapped. She perched on the edge of the red velvet seat, ready for anything. Gondolas with a *felze* were rare. This one must be quite old. The roof of the cabin was quilted with gold damask, the fittings brass. 'I hope this trip costs you a fortune,' she said sourly.

Fiorenzo smiled to himself and sat opposite her. 'I'm sure it will. But it'll be worth it. Go on, then, let's see how you convince me that I shouldn't harass a woman who's committed almost every crime in the book.'

'Don't lie to me. I know you're making it all up,' said Suzy hotly. 'You're hitting her where it hurts most.'

'That's right. Through her pride and her son. Of course I am. I want to do the maximum damage.'

He sounded unmoved. The gondola glided beneath the Bridge of Sighs which joined the massive stone walls of the fourteenth-century Doge's Palace with the old courtrooms. Suzy suddenly felt a foreboding, as if she was trapped just like the condemned criminals, the prisoners of long ago, who'd made that journey across the bridge and seen Venice for the last time through its tiny windows.

She moved along the seat. Fiorenzo's arm lay across the back and he was smiling at her. It was the smile of a hungry man who smelled supper cooking.

'The Contessa has told me that you're threatening to publicise a scandal,' she said, trying to keep her voice even. 'One that isn't even true. Why? In order to acquire a palace you can't afford to run? Don't you think you'd look a little ridiculous in it?'

'I'm sure I could learn to strut as easily as Guido does,' he replied in an amused voice.

Suzy tried not to acknowledge to herself the fact that he'd look better than the real prince. 'What about your right to be there? Could you honestly live with yourself, knowing that you'd turned out its rightful occupant? The Moroschini have been there since the twelfth century.'

'I could live with myself,' he said implacably. 'You're not putting your passion to good use. Trying to persuade me that Flavia needs charitable sympathy is a waste of time. Shift your passion in my direction. I know what to do with it.' His hand idly stroked her shoulder. She jerked away and persevered.

'She's confined to a wheelchair, maybe for the rest of her life. Can't you dredge up an ounce of compassion for her?'

'Did Guido send you?' he asked mildly, totally ignoring her again.

'No,' she said irritably. Fiorenzo's hand brushed the side of her cheek and she flinched. No, quivered. She frowned, hoping he hadn't appreciated the difference.

His finger and thumb played with her earlobe. She jerked her head away in a sharp movement. 'Nice little ears,' he mused. 'Guido didn't ask you to use your feminine wiles on me, as you did yesterday?'

Suzy gulped. 'Yesterday? You're talking nonsense——'

'Am I? You've known all along who I was, and yet you were charming to me. Is that a normal response? Fluttering your lashes...?' He caught her hand. 'Allowing me to kiss your soft palm and admire your long, painted nails, so that I could discover you had never washed up much more than...oh, a handful of dishes...'

'Oh.' Now she knew what had been nagging at her.

'Yes,' he said, his eyes gleaming. 'Oh, Suzy, I don't take kindly to people lying to me. I don't take kindly to attempts on my life by ruthless Contessas, either,' he added with soft, heart-stopping menace. 'God knows where she got the money to borrow a police launch and bribe an assassin.'

Her head swivelled around and she stared at him in frank disbelief. 'You can't imagine...? That's crazy! You're accusing the Contessa of employing some kind of hit-man? She wouldn't——'

'Really? Do you know the stakes, Suzy?'

'Stakes?'

Fiorenzo cradled her chin in his big hand and his face came to within an inch of hers. He was allowing her to see inside him, to the hard steel core. Fiorenzo believed he was in danger of his life, that was clear, and so his behaviour had escalated to a point where he would do anything to crush Flavia and Guido. Her flesh crawled. He'd crush her, too, as casually as if treading on an ant beneath his feet. There was a clamminess about her palms. She wiped them surreptitiously on her thighs.

Trapped by his warm hand, she felt the contrasting iciness of her face as he blasted her with his freezing, glacial eyes. And she was frozen with fear.

'The stakes are the future,' he said softly. 'Flavia's, Guido's, mine. And I intend to put my own interests first. Want to know what I'm going to do? Shake Flavia's comfortable little world. I'm going to take possession of that palace.'

'It belongs to Prince Moroschini!' she reminded him coldly.

'It certainly does.'

'Then let him stay there!' she cried.

'I intend to.'

Suzy glared at him in exasperation. 'Guido——'

'Oh, we're talking about *Guido*,' he said, as if the penny had dropped. 'I'm more of a prince than he is,' went on Fiorenzo scornfully. 'Do you know who his *real* father is? Any idea why Flavia's husband left her? Not many men take kindly to being cuckolded.'

'Is that what you're claiming?' Suzy asked in astonishment.

'That's the truth. Guido's a bastard. So now you see how tenuous Flavia's position is. One word from me about Guido's parentage, and she'll lose everything she has. That's why the stakes are high, and why she tried to arrange a fatal accident for me.'

Behind them, the gondolier called a warning cry as he negotiated a blind corner, swinging the boat around with a swerve of his hips and a thrust of the pole as he manoeuvred the gondola into a one-way system—and going

the wrong way himself. Suzy trawled for her scattered
wits. Had she been going the wrong way, too? Fiorenzo
sounded so plausible. It was a convincing story. A
dreadful suspicion crawled into her mind. It would explain her private opinion about the way Guido looked.
But the bit about the Contessa being a murderess was
impossible to believe. Fiorenzo had overstated his case.

The gondola moved silently beneath a high-arched
bridge, its undersides flecked with water reflections. No.
It was all clear to her. She dismissed her doubts. The
unfortunate Contessa Flavia was above suspicion and
this man was a liar. 'You're paranoid,' she said into his
harsh face, feeling her breath bounce back.

'Like hell I am!' he snarled, grabbing her arms and
shaking her. 'Think, woman! Why does Alfonso remain
in Flavia's employ, even though he isn't paid?'

'Alfonso?' she gasped. 'You're suggesting he's Guido's
real father? Are you mad? He stays because he has
loyalty. Because he respects Flavia Moroschini, and
perhaps feels pity for her.'

'She works on that pity,' ground out Fiorenzo. 'She
always has used feminine tricks to get what she wants.
All right. So you fondly imagine that Alfonso is noble-
minded and loyal. Might he stay for another reason?
Does he still look at her secretly? Does he still hand her
in and out of the launch as if she were a queen? Does
her smile linger affectionately on him——?'

'Stop!' she cried in horror. 'I won't listen——'

Her furious cry was stifled as he clamped his mouth
on hers, pressing her back in the seat and trapping her
with his whole weight.

'Shut up and think, damn you!' he muttered angrily
against her bruised mouth. Freed, she immediately
reached out to bite him. He ducked away swiftly.
'Think!' he repeated. 'Just stop yelling and spend a few
moments seeing if what I say could be true.'

'I won't! It's disgusting! You can't possibly imagine that anyone would take you seriously?' Suzy cried, aghast. The haughty Flavia, and Alfonso? It was too ludicrous for words.

'Of course they would,' he said nastily. 'The whole of Venice would be thrilled to believe it. You said yourself that Guido looked like a peasant.'

'I—you're twisting my words! Oh, God! Is there nothing we can do to stop you spreading this disgusting rumour?' asked Suzy grimly.

His mocking eyes flicked over her. 'Oh, I'm sure you'll think of something,' he murmured, his hand insolently slipping inside her coat to cup her breast. She shut her eyes in disgust and suffered his touch. 'I can't wait to engage in a full-scale battle with you,' he growled.

'Good Lord, you're playing "the heavy" again,' she said wearily. 'I told you. If you're trying to frighten me, you've picked the wrong woman. I don't panic if a man yells at me. I yell back. Or bite. Or wait till he realises I'm bored.'

He'd stop soon. If she made no response, he'd leave her alone. The private gondola had become a prison. She couldn't fight him, or cause a fuss, because it could overturn and she'd end up in the canal. He'd outwitted her again, damn him!

'Let me run this by you again. Leave me alone. Stop following me, and I won't do anything to hurt you. Don't side with Flavia. You'll get nothing from her—especially money. She's in debt up to her aristocratic eyeballs.'

'You're making that up! She's already paid my advance. Besides, you can't possibly know——'

'Oh, I've oiled a lot of wheels over the past four months,' he said smoothly. 'Enough to create a slick that would turn the Grand Canal black. I know her financial situation intimately. Why back a losing horse? What has she ever done for you?'

'I'll tell you what she's done! She set me up in business. Not financially, but she gave me a building to work in,' asserted Suzy defiantly. 'If that isn't generous, I don't know what is.'

'Very generous. How long ago?'

'Not long. A few months.'

'Neat. The very moment she needs a tame detective. The woman earns my admiration. I must watch my back. So you're going to help your benefactress.'

'Of course I'll stick by the Contessa,' she said vehemently. 'I'm loyal too. And I'll open a bottle of champagne when you're thrown into prison.'

'You'll get thirsty waiting. I must say, you leave me with mixed feelings,' he mused. 'I'm half glad, half sorry you won't bow out of the scene. Mind you, it'll be more fun grinding you into the ground than crushing Flavia and Guido.' His lips parted and his tongue touched one corner of his mouth as he contemplated his revenge. 'And the sex will be earth-shattering——'

Suzy leapt forwards in fury, intending to get out of the cabin and take her chances with the canal. The boat rocked. Fiorenzo's foot stretched out and she slammed into the seat opposite, falling in an undignified and slightly winded heap on the thick red carpet, her coat flying open.

'Oh, joy, oh, rapture,' he murmured in her ear. 'We're having a little tumble together again.' Her arm flew up to ward him off, but his body crushed down on her with unnerving intimacy. 'It's one way to keep warm,' he said cheerfully, shifting his pelvis a little. 'Friction. Didn't I learn something about friction when I was a boy scout?'

'The scout movement has more sense than to let a wolf into its cub pack,' she snapped, daunted by the hot, male pressure on her loins. He was hard and aroused, the virile throb between them making her eyes widen in alarm. He shifted again, to emphasise his sexuality, and she felt her eyes closing of their own volition in sensual pleasure. 'The gondolier!' she husked.

'Don't worry,' murmured Fiorenzo. 'I paid him so much that he'd turn a blind eye if we stripped naked and went through every position in the *Karma Sutra*.' He touched her hair tentatively.

'Don't touch me!' she shrieked.

'Frightened?' he taunted huskily.

She was, terrified. And so she used her sharp tongue to slash him. 'No wonder your own father loathed you!' she grated.

Fiorenzo went quite still. It was like hitting the centre of a storm. For in that brief pause, the frozen silence, Suzy became aware of a wild flame of temper being remorselessly harnessed—for the time being. He slid off her and sat on the seat opposite while she stared at him from the floor like a hypnotised rabbit. She felt ashamed of herself. Fear had made her cruel.

In his eyes was a blistering hatred of her, of the whole world, it seemed. And she knew instinctively that he wouldn't stop until he'd fatally wounded Flavia and Guido and herself.

'My God! You can wound a man with those soft lips of yours.'

'I'm sorry——'

'I bet you are. Didn't mean to make me really angry, did you? If you wanted to dissuade me, you've failed. Flavia might think she's been through hell,' he breathed, his eyes glittering with missionary zeal, 'but she ain't seen nothin' yet. I'm about to introduce her to it. When I'm finished with her, there'll be nowhere in Italy she can go. People will treat her like a leper. You can tell her that it is my intention that she suffers *exactly* as I have suffered. Blow for blow. I've been planning this ever since I was old enough to think.'

Suzy felt her body turn ice cold. His head had tipped back in challenge, the scrolling nostrils flaring in warning. He was obsessed. His mind was turned.

'You're sick,' she whispered. 'You need help.'

'So will you,' he said softly. *'May God help you.'*

Suzy shrank against the seat. He sat looking out of the window like a carved statue, his hard profile as bleak as the snowy scene outside. She began to shiver uncontrollably, and still trembled when he stopped the gondola and lifted her out by C'a Priuli, giving her a little push when she didn't move.

Chilled by her encounter with Fiorenzo, Suzy tried to shake off the feeling of menace which curled around her as she walked home, particularly when she entered a *sottoportego*. The dark walkways, running like tunnels beneath the houses, were sinister enough under normal circumstances. Today she wanted to keep looking over her shoulder, to see if he was following, but her pride wouldn't let her. Whatever she pretended to the contrary, he had frightened her. He was a fanatic. He could do anything.

And she had failed. Miserably.

The snow had stopped. Venice lay cold and glittering, inhabited by brightly costumed figures taking advantage of the kinder weather to display their originality. Hooded figures slipped through the alleys, wolves and hobgoblins turned every corner. And Suzy jumped with fright each time she bumped into someone, causing the wolves and hobgoblins, the highwaymen and bewigged aristocrats to laugh and exchange amused comments in all the languages of the world.

Cursing the Carnival, Suzy morosely packed a case and took it to the palace. Her room in the attic was small and cramped, with only a tiny window to let in the winter light. She glanced around at the sparse furniture and tried not to mind. She was doing this for Flavia—and in any case, it didn't matter where she slept. A lot of her time would be spent in the palace itself. That was some consolation. The palace might be run-down, but it still held a magic that enthralled and delighted her.

She wandered around the rooms, trying in vain to be enthralled and delighted. She'd tried to find Flavia or Guido, to tell them what had happened, but they were nowhere around. Suzy pinned her faith on the note Flavia was sending to Fiorenzo. He might shelve his operations for a while. It would give her some breathing space.

Early that afternoon she set off for the Lido, with Alfonso driving the Moroschini launch. It had been carefully hoovered, brasses polished, windows cleaned till they sparkled.

Alfonso squirmed in a hastily pressed medieval boatman's costume and looked very uncomfortable. But she . . . ! Flavia had left her instructions to wear a low-cut Botticelli gown, laced with pearls and gold thread, the full moss-green satin skirts slowing her movements, her head reduced to careful, graceful gestures by the pearls which threaded her loose hair.

Suzy pulled the hood of her cloak around her head as she stood on the boat, hoping she wouldn't meet anyone she knew. And praying that Mr Verreaux didn't expect any 'favours' from his interpreter-cum-hostess.

The lagoon was like grey silk, each small island rising from it like a jewel dusted with snow. Suzy turned to look back at Venice and felt the tug of possession in her heart. No wonder the Contessa had been in despair at the thought of abandoning her home. It was the most beautiful city in the world. And Fiorenzo must not take possession of the palace. He didn't belong there, not with his sour, stark hatred and pagan appetites.

Alfonso began to sing to himself quietly, an old waterman's song, and she sighed. It would all be perfect, if it wasn't for Fiorenzo.

Reaching the Lido di Venezia, they motored gently down the coast of the island and into a high-banked canal. It opened dramatically into the basin which served as a land entrance for the creeper-clad Hotel Excelsior. Suzy knew of it, and that it was a turn-of-the-century building, but she'd had no idea how lovely it was, sitting with stately grandeur in lush gardens, the slender turrets and the elegant façade mirrored in the clear water.

Alfonso was directed to tie up to one of the striped *bricole*. Seeing the eyes of the tail-coated porter on him, and the crew of the hotel boat, he skulked down in the cabin while Suzy stepped carefully on to the jetty. Many of the guests were in costume, so she didn't feel out of place, though she did mind their eyes lingering on her deeply plunging neckline. She squirmed inside, thinking she must look like a saucy wench, promoting a medieval banquet.

'*Signor Verreaux, quando arriverà?*' she said to the man in the upstairs reception foyer, asking when the banker would arrive.

'*Giù dalle scale.*' The man pointed to the lower hall where she'd come in, and she hurried back. Already there in the hall were four massive suitcases labelled with Verreaux's name, stacked near a desk, but no sign of the American himself.

'You're looking for someone?' asked the tail-coated porter in perfect English.

She smiled to herself ruefully, admiring his instant identification of her nationality. 'Yes. Mr Verreaux.'

'He will not be a moment. If you would wait by his luggage?'

She stood by the cases, feeling conspicuous. Outside on the jetty, in a warm afternoon sun, a toddler was reaching down with a toy gondola in his hands, his elegantly suited father cautiously clutching the waistband of the little boy's trousers. But she paid no attention to the man, other than vaguely registering his presence, because her eyes were softly fixed on the little boy as he tenderly placed the boat on the water while indulgent staff all around her paused to watch.

The child's face lit up with joy when the gondola floated, and he trailed it up and down on its string as if it was infinitely precious.

A child. She had wanted one more than anything in the world. So had Mario. He'd also wanted sex and food, as often as possible. Exhausted from providing both, and from working a long day in the insurance office, Suzy had been in no fit state to become a mother at the age of almost nineteen. Her miscarriages had temporarily ruined her health and, after her divorce, had made her hesitate to get involved with another man.

All she could do was to be an onlooker, to envy the children of other people. Captivated by the little boy outside, Suzy moved nearer to the entrance as the child solemnly lifted the boat out of the water and earnestly flicked water from its precious hull.

Tears blurred her eyes. Her babies would have been toddlers now. They'd been so small when they'd died, so defenceless. And she'd been to blame, according to Mario. Her tears had bored him. She was useless, he had said. For what Italian man wanted a wife who could produce no living sons?

Through her softly veiled eyes, she saw the man outside lift the child and throw him exuberantly into the air, the weak sun-rays beaming down on them both in approval.

Suzy blinked. Then she pulled a handkerchief from her pocket, dabbed her eyes. Froze, when her eyes confirmed what she already knew. The father of the little boy was Fiorenzo Veronese.

This was Veronese transformed, as she'd never seen him before—joyous, open, laughing, teasing. He was tickling his son and evoking generous sighs from the nearby porters and hotel boatmen, who seemed to feel no shame in showing their tender hearts.

Nor, apparently, did Fiorenzo. Suzy's head pounded with the astounding discovery. She couldn't believe that a man could look so different. Her eyes devoured him, her heart lurching wildly at his yearning and adoring expression, all the more poignant because it mirrored her own. If she were an artist, only hours ago she would have portrayed him with a cold, haughty profile, because it was so deeply impressed on her mind. But now even his chiselled cheekbones seemed less austere, and his mouth just burst with laughter and affectionate words of worship as he nuzzled his evidently adored son.

It struck her as infinitely sad and it tore at her heart that he was a deeply caring, potentially loving man, eaten up by envy. He had a son. He could abandon his vengeance and still be happy—he didn't know how lucky he was.

There was a muttering behind Suzy and the reporters leapt to the assistance of a stunningly beautiful woman, groomed to the last eyelash, who strode assertively through the door in a waft of expensive perfume. The woman received a bow from Fiorenzo and the little boy. Fiorenzo kissed her hand, gallantly helped her into a waiting hotel launch, and lifted in the child, watching them leave with a wistful look on his face that made Suzy wince.

Married; the proof before her. A swooping dismay hollowed her stomach. She groaned silently that she should be affected. But that beautiful woman owned not only his body, but his heart and soul; she had made him happy with the very product of sexual unity—a son.

Why that should make her want to throw things, she didn't know. But...he was a callous swine, to make a pass at her, when he was already spoken for! Rat, rat, *rat*! Anger filled Suzy with sour emotion. He'd seen her as a casual bit of fun, something to give vent to his passions.

She frowned. Why was he camping out in a tenement, if he was married to a rich goddess? Why was he dressed now as if he owned Gianfranco Ferre? Why...

Panic-stricken, Suzy darted behind a potted palm with a rustle of her skirts. Fiorenzo was coming inside. Fervently she prayed that he'd leave before the banker arrived. Botticelli women looked ridiculous hiding behind overgrown plants. She moved back a little into the recess and discovered that her pearl-strewn hair had caught somehow on a frond. If she moved, he'd spot her. Damn! It was like a stage farce.

He murmured something to the porter. The porter murmured something back. Fiorenzo looked startled, and headed straight for Suzy's plant. She tried desperately to look like part of the scenery, but Fiorenzo prowled around the palm tree to see what kind of creature would hide in the undergrowth.

He lifted the fronds and his puzzled face broke into a wolfish grin when he saw Suzy's flushed and sullen face. Slowly, with elaborate care, his eyes toured her costume while she tried in vain to untangle her hair from the palm, only succeeding in wriggling the cloak from her shoulders. She stared in dismay at it, wishing she could free herself and reach down to cover herself up. Looking like a refugee from an amateur dramatic production was putting her at a disadvantage.

'You want to be careful, exposing your chest to the elements,' he smiled, his eyes dancing. 'Look, it's covered in goose-bumps.' His palm lay flat on her breast, warm, welcome. Suzy shuddered and drew back as far as she could, right into the corner where no one could see her, wincing when her hair pulled her short by tugging at the roots. 'Allow me,' he murmured in amusement. 'Pearls play hell with one's hair, don't they?'

Hiding her fear, she glowered as he stepped up to her, his feet treading firmly on her long dress and trapping her still further. His broad back successfully blocked her from sight of anyone in Reception. A few inches away, his body seemed all heat and carnality, flowing over her and making her feel giddy.

'Go away,' she muttered, fiddling with her hair. 'I'm waiting for someone.'

'Casanova, by the looks of you.'

'That rules you out, then.'

He grinned, reaching up and spending a long time un-hooking her, his warm breath whispering erotically over her mouth. Then he bent and kissed her bare neck, the suddenness and unexpectedness of it making her gasp in delight.

'No——'

'Yes,' he said, in a muted growl, appraising her con-fused face. 'Intoxicating, isn't it? I would never have believed how exciting sexual revenge could be. We're going to enjoy this.'

She tried to move, but he stood squarely on her ex-pensive skirt. 'Off!' she seethed. 'Or I'll scream!'

He shrugged, his hand hypnotically caressing her neck. 'I don't care. Scream if you want.'

She dared not, because the must-be-impressed Mr Verreaux might trot down at any moment to claim his luggage. So she jammed her forearm up to catch his chin and knock him off balance. It was met by his vice-hard grip.

'Leave me alone, you bully!' She glared as he hauled her arching body against his.

'Oh, pretty,' he mocked. 'Those big, saucer-like green eyes. What are you all got up for?' His eyes dropped to her cleavage pressed provocatively against his chest, and his expression became cold. 'Is Flavia offering you to some visiting Arab? Have you agreed to be some rich man's darling?'

Suzy tried to see over Fiorenzo's shoulder. As far as she could tell, no one had come down. Verreaux was late, thank goodness. 'It's only a costume,' she said edgily. 'You've had your two-pennyworth of looking. Now disappear.'

'Kiss me and I will.'

Her eyes rolled skywards. 'Your technique is incredibly retarded,' she said scathingly. 'The boys at school used to say that to me when they caught me. We were five at the time,' she reminisced. 'Go and play with someone your own mental age and size!'

His eyes laughed down at her. 'I missed out on that kind of game. I missed out on any games as a child. So I must play them now—and I don't mind your being my mental inferior. At least you are my size,' he said triumphantly. 'Haven't you noticed? The way we fit together?' He moved his body against hers, the pressure of heat surging hard and exquisitely urgent between them.

'This is ridiculous——!'

'Kiss me.'

He stood there, defiantly, a mocking smile on his face. It was time his ego was taken down a peg or two.

'Oh, God! I was hoping I wouldn't have to do this again. Let's get it over with,' she said with heavy boredom.

Suzy tightened her mouth into an impenetrable barrier over her teeth, and reached up in the direction of his amused lips. His hand clamped on the back of her head, but he kept an inch or two away from her unwilling mouth, his eyes lazily watching her, the flare of his nostrils and the spread of his blackening pupils making her legs weak. And all the time her heart was pounding because his hand was sliding up her tight bodice, over her rib-cage, cupping under the soft curve of her breast, touching the thin silk fichu which covered her bosom. Her breasts jutted out to beg for his hand. Still his mouth hovered. Suzy swallowed and her mouth quavered, breaking the hard, relentless line she had shaped it into.

Then he kissed her, with a tender sweetness that made her want to yell. Her body pulsed to the slow, steady rhythm of his hand rubbing her nipple. It became hard, tight, painful. And then he had taken a step back.

'Who are you waiting for?' he asked a little shakily. His eyes gleamed with a fierce excitement and it was all Suzy could do to hold her turbulent body in check. A crazy wanting poured through her like a flash-flood.

She flung her head up in defiance. 'None of your business.'

'Tell me,' he coaxed. He possessed her mouth with a sweetness that sent spirals of exhilaration spinning around her head. She melted inside as the flames of desire consumed her.

Tactics, she thought blearily. Take him by surprise. As if in desperation to assuage her need for the touch of his body, she wriggled against him, placing her hands on his shoulders and trying to stand on tiptoe as if wanting to reach his mouth. His lips smiled with a triumphant surprise beneath hers. She pulled on her dress, which was preventing her from coming closer, and he moved from it, kicking it away from his feet to help her line her body against his.

She'd fooled him! Released at last, she darted away, into the hall and safety.

Almost whimpering with anger, she waited, aware that the porters had noticed her flushed, dishevelled appearance, and were valiantly trying not to snicker. With her head held high she gritted her teeth and stuck it out. Verreaux would come soon. Please, make it soon. There was an emptiness in her that she had to release on someone, something. A wild frenzy, an intoxication that made her want to yell or cry, or both. Oh, God! What was he doing to her?

Fiorenzo emerged from the palm fronds and watched her for a few interminable seconds, standing negligently by the counter. She could see him out of the corner of her eye, though she pretended she wasn't paying him any attention. He straightened his tie, slicked a hand over his unruly waves to smooth them, and checked his cuffs. Then he had the gall to push his shirt more firmly into his trousers.

Humiliation flooded through her as the porters snickered. She hadn't... Had she? Her face was brick-red, she knew, testifying to her guilt. And *he* had the appearance of a man who'd been with a whore. Grimly she wondered what was worse than castration. When she thought of it, he'd have it.

He flicked an imperious finger at a porter. Three of them leapt forwards—and picked up the luggage belonging to Mr Verreaux.

'Wait a minute! You can't do that!' Suzy cried angrily. There was no way he could know who she was waiting for.

'Buon viaggo, Signor Verreaux,' called the head porter with stately dignity, wishing Fiorenzo a good trip.

Fiorenzo? Verreaux? Signor... Suzy's eyes closed in prayer. Let it not be him. Life couldn't possibly be that cruel.

'Shall we go?' asked Fiorenzo calmly. 'I believe you're waiting for me.'

Her huge green eyes snapped open to take a startled look at his devastatingly expensive dark grey suit and shoes, the immaculately shot white cuffs with their gold links. The smoothly shaved face. The beautifully groomed hair. The air of arrogant hauteur. Deferential porters. Verreaux.

'*Verreaux?*' Her voice croaked hoarsely. He was. She could tell that by the grin on his face and the light of victory in his eyes. Her shoulders slumped. 'What exactly do you think you're doing?' she asked wearily.

'Isn't that obvious? I'm on my way to stay at the *palazzo* for three months.'

Her head shot up. 'You must be mad! We won't let you——'

'"We." You identify with her. Goddam you, Green Eyes,' he said softly.

'Me? What have I done? My God, you pretend to be a rich American banker——'

'I *am* a rich American banker,' said Fiorenzo coolly.

'Oh, yes? First you're a Swiss citizen with an Italian name and a Surrey accent, and now you're a wealthy American called *Verreaux?*' she accused. 'God, you're a liar!'

'I said I came from Switzerland, which is true. I do have an Italian name. I learned English from my nurse. I am an American banker,' he said with a detached smile.

'You're not American!'

'Never said I was. I *said* I was an American banker. There's a subtle difference. You see, I own a bank in New York. Actually,' he said in a confidential manner, 'I also own one in London and one in Switzerland, too, but I don't like to boast about them.'

'It gets better,' she scathed. 'You must be the only wealthy banker who rents cheap apartments and goes around in unlabelled denim and—and underwear that——' She stopped. As soon as she'd said that, she realised he'd been fooling them all, pretending to be poor for some devious reason. After all, he was hardly wearing rags now.

'My goodness, I didn't know you'd investigated me so thoroughly,' he mocked. But his eyes were hard and glittering, and his mouth tight with menace.

'I don't understand. I went through everything in your flat,' she grated. 'You have hardly a penny to your name.'

'I went through everything in yours,' he said coldly. 'And you're desperate for money, aren't you? That photocopier cost you a fortune. I could have got you one cheaper.'

She went white. And then saw the funny side of it. They'd been turning over each other's belongings at the same time. Her mouth twisted into a wry smile. 'All right,' she said defiantly. 'The joke is over. What's your game?'

'I freely admit I've lied and cheated my way into leasing the *palazzo*. I admit I've been renting a cheap apartment and going around in nondescript clothes. I can't remember there being a law against that. But thank God that's over.' His hand stroked the beautiful material of his lapel. 'I have a very Italian dislike of badly cut garments.'

'Over?' she frowned. 'What do you mean?'

'My poverty was temporary. A necessary subterfuge. I didn't want Flavia to know everything about me. If she'd realised I had money, she'd have fleeced me of it and *then* dumped me in the canal. Did you enjoy those churches we visited, you and me? Personally I found them boring.'

'You knew you were being followed?' she asked, unable to hide her disappointment.

'Only because I was expecting it,' he said comfortingly. 'I'd seen Alfonso prowling around at the airport, you see. It isn't easy for a big man like that to hide behind potted palms.' He grinned. 'Flavia must have found your reports on me very boring. All that sightseeing and sitting in cafés—sometimes I almost leapt up to invite you in. You must have been so cold, hopping about outside from one foot to another,' he added, sounding insincerely sympathetic.

Suzy let out a heavy, infuriated breath. 'Go on,' she said coldly. 'I'm loathing you more and more with every word you utter.'

'I did say I had a superior intelligence,' he murmured smugly.

'Oh, I haven't finished with you yet,' she said grimly. 'You're rich? Really a banker?'

'Ah, the gleam in a woman's eye when she links money with a man,' he grinned. 'I'm disgustingly rich. I can afford gondolas with cabins and even Flavia's exorbitant rent. Now I do think we ought to go. Alfonso will be wondering if you've been playing Mummies and Daddies in your American banker's suite.'

Quite dazed, she made no protest when he propelled her out of the hall to the jetty. 'Why pretend to be staying here?' she frowned.

'It's no pretence. I've had a suite here all the time. It was booked some time ago and all my luggage was sent here. You see, I was very anxious to make an impressive entrance when I arrived at the palace. I did want to look my best, returning triumphant after six long years. Flavia will be stunned, don't you think?' he said cheerfully.

'Stunned,' Suzy agreed sardonically, feeling sick.

She was very pale, her eyes a dark forest-green in her appalled face. But she held herself proudly and struggled to get her mind into gear. There must be something she could do. Seeing Fiorenzo arrive in grand state would give the Contessa hysterics.

'God!' sighed Fiorenzo. 'It's good to feel silk next to the skin again. You'll adore my proper underwear. Like you, I'm very sensitive to touch, Suzy.'

'I've noticed,' she said curtly, wishing he wouldn't keep distracting her thoughts.

'Oh, good. You'll know how to please me.'

'Is your wife staying with you?' she asked coolly, suppressing the desire to grit her teeth in anger. That would please him too much, and she never, ever wanted to do that.

'My wife? Me, married? You don't think I'd tie myself down to one woman, do you?' he asked in frank amazement. 'Charm over the cornflakes? Tenderness at teatime, exchanges of emotion? Not my style, Suzy. You're my kind of girl, no hang-ups, a wild enjoyment of sex——'

'I've seen the child, I've seen the wife,' she cut in sharply. 'Don't lie about *everything* as a matter of principle, Fiorenzo. Know when to have the grace to stop.'

'The child... Oh!' He grinned broadly as if something amused him. 'How appearances can be deceptive,' he said smoothly. 'Things are *never* what they seem, are they? You must remember that, Suzy, if you're to progress in your job. Always assume the impossible.'

'Thanks for the advice,' she replied drily. 'The child?'

'Oh, yes. I was only keeping an eye on him while his mother returned to her room for something she'd forgotten.'

'It was a very enthusiastic eye,' she reminded him, wanting him to acknowledge his brief tenderness.

He lifted a cynical eyebrow. 'Looked convincing, did it? I hoped to impress the mother,' he drawled. 'Gorgeous, wasn't she? Adore a woman's son and she's yours.'

'You do find it easy being a bastard, don't you?' she said evenly. 'I wonder why you chose the name Verreaux? It's not even remotely American. Why not Ripper, or Frankenstein?'

'What a sharp little tongue you have,' he mocked. 'I must watch it when I kiss you. It could lacerate my throat.'

'It would never get anywhere near your throat!' she snapped.

'Challenge,' he murmured teasingly. 'If you want to know, Verreaux is the name of a large black eagle—and the Moroschini emblem is an eagle. Verreaux's eagle is a bird of prey, Suzy—rare, very special, living in splendid isolation in desolate surroundings. It's quite lethal where the local population of small mammals is concerned. Wipes them out. Rather apt, don't you think?'

She stared at him cynically. 'David Attenborough would be proud of you. What are you up to?'

'The eagle has landed. I'm taking over the palace,' he said softly. 'Even if I've paid in advance for the pleasure. No matter. I intend to make the most of it.'

'You can't *stay*!' she cried in amazement. 'When the Contessa sees it's you, she'll get Alfonso to throw you out!'

'I don't think so.' Fiorenzo's mouth curved into a contemptuous sneer. 'You see, I'm the only man who stands between her and prison. I could turn a few screws and happily watch her being taken away for evasion of taxes. And...there's the exciting news about Alfonso which is on the tip of my tongue. It's so difficult not to share it with someone. Speaking of which, shall we go and surprise him?'

His forceful grip on her arm drove her reluctantly the few feet to the Moroschini launch, where Alfonso was stacking the suitcases. Fiorenzo stood motionless on the jetty with Suzy a virtual prisoner beside him. After a moment Alfonso saw Fiorenzo's knife-tailored legs and leapt ashore. And turned a sickly green at the sight of Fiorenzo.

'*Il Principe!*' he gasped hoarsely.

'How nice that someone still knows who the hell I am,' drawled Fiorenzo.

'You're a prince, like Guido?' Suzy asked in surprise.

'Not quite like Guido. I am *Il Principe Fiorenzo Veronese Corradino Moroschini*, Knight of St Sophia.

That should get me a table at Florian's, don't you think?'
he murmured. 'I suppose I'll have to get a specially large
visiting-card printed, to get all that on.'

'How are you a prince? As Guido's distant cousin?'
she asked, puzzled.

He gave her an enigmatic smile as if he was enjoying
himself hugely. 'Alfonso, *pronto*? He's ready. Get on
the boat, Suzy. I'm looking forward to the next hour.'

'You can't do this to the Contessa!' she breathed in
horror, as he bundled her into the cabin unceremoni-
ously. 'Please don't! Alfonso!' she called over her
shoulder. 'Help! *Mi aiuti!*'

'He daren't,' said Fiorenzo curtly. 'He's terrified of
me. And so should you be.' He pulled her close, as the
boat surged away from the jetty and Suzy found herself
staring up at his savage face, all his cool detachment
vanished now. 'You accuse me of deception,' he snarled,
'but you were part of that plan last night, weren't you?
Lord, I could shake the living daylights out of you! I
know you're hard up and in Flavia's debt, but your
morals alone ought to have stopped you from getting
involved.'

'I don't know what you're talking about!' she yelled.

'Hard as nails, aren't you?' he said bitterly, shoving
her back so that she fell on to the deep, buttoned
cushions. 'And that won't work, either,' he roared,
reaching forwards and pulling up her bodice, which had
released most of her breasts from the fichu.

She felt weak and ill, impaled by his disgust and contempt. 'I wasn't—you're wrong——!'

'Like hell I am! You were Plan B, weren't you?
Swinging sweetly into operation when Plan A didn't work
and I emerged from the canal unscathed.'

'No!' she cried in horror. 'You can't accuse me
of...of... I don't believe this!' she breathed.

'Neither do I. I've no idea why you didn't slit my throat while I slept,' he said scathingly.

'Maybe I wish I had,' she snapped. 'It would have saved us a lot of trouble.'

'Oh, now we have it,' he seethed. 'Tell me what you're getting out of it! A liaison with Guido? Don't imagine for one minute that you'll hook him permanently. He might want to marry you after romping in bed with you, but he'll obey his mother in all things. Flavia would never let a little nobody marry her precious little darling.'

'Of course I have no intention of any emotional—or physical—relationship with Guido!' she cried furiously.

'You're a liar,' Fiorenzo said harshly. 'I saw his hot eyes on you.'

'You're imagining things. Can't you believe that I care about justice——'

'Justice?' he roared, catching hold of her arms. He looked so utterly forbidding that her knees gave way momentarily. Roughly he held her up, the wild flame of temper coming remorselessly under control. 'Justice?' he mocked. 'If there's any of that in this world, Flavia would be selling matches on the street!'

'In her wheelchair?' Suzy suggested with blistering scorn. She extracted herself from his grip by unpeeling his fingers one by one and, without another word, she went out to sit by Alfonso. His hands were shaking uncontrollably on the wheel. She tried to talk to him but he remained silent, his face ghastly.

In distress, she stood shivering in the chilly wind as they sped across the lagoon towards the tiny city of Venice. A weak sun had emerged, promising an end to the snow. As the pale orange globe sank in the west, the water sparkled with pink, red and gold. If a hurricane blew up, she wouldn't go below to share the cabin with

Fiorenzo. She didn't know what he intended to do, but it would be something awful, she knew. There was more anger and revenge in that man's heart than she could ever have believed possible.

CHAPTER SIX

THE Doge's Palace came into view. The usual thrill that Suzy felt at seeing it was no longer there. The fabulous Salute church, built on a million wooden stakes. Elegant, crumbling palaces where Wagner and Byron had worked, where Churchill, Dürer, kings and emperors had stayed. Tantalising glimpses of rooms decorated by Titian, Tintoretto, Michelangelo, jammed together in glorious array, gazing serenely on the silent gondolas, the barges and ferries, the bustling water-buses and gliding *sandali*.

For her it was a terrible journey. For Veronese, she thought, it must be thrilling. Short of sinking the launch with them all in it, she couldn't come up with anything to stop him from his confrontation with the Contessa. Closer and closer with every second came the Palazzo Moroschini, and she knew with a sinking heart that Guido and the Contessa would be waiting at the watergate, decked out in their Sunday best, excited, relaxed, ready to welcome their guest. Instead, they'd come face to face with the man they hated and feared, and who meant to overturn their lives.

'Stand off! *Si fermi qui!*'

Alfonso obeyed Fiorenzo's sharp command from below and held the launch steady in the water just opposite to the palace. Suzy guiltily looked at the two smartly dressed figures on the jetty smiling and waving, and the two white blodges in the shadowy doorway which were probably the aprons worn by the maid and the cook.

All nice and ready to receive the American Who Must Be Impressed.

She groaned. Alfonso spat expressively into the canal. She knew how he felt.

Flavia and Guido couldn't see Fiorenzo. They'd be thinking that the American had ordered Alfonso to stop the launch so that he could admire the building.

It was a nightmare situation. Flavia had been thrilled, talking about her plans for the future. Suzy heaved a deep, despairing sigh. Her eyes were drawn as if by a magnet to Fiorenzo. Under her lashes, she saw that he'd raised his head out of the hatchway, just enough to see the palace without being seen himself.

'Fiorenzo——' she began huskily.

'Be silent.' His words were barely audible. She'd expected him to show triumph, a bitter vengeance, perhaps elation. Instead his face was impassive.

She scrutinised him minutely. And noticed one or two tell-tale details about him. The veins in his temples were standing out. The hands which gripped the top of the hatch were white-knuckled. The whole of his body seemed stiff. He was tense, as if this meeting held more meaning for him than she knew.

It was interesting that he was a prince—so he said. Certainly Alfonso had acknowledged that. Her eyes narrowed. The rivalry between Fiorenzo and Guido had something to do with inheritance. And she wished she'd never got involved. It hurt her to see families at war. They had no idea what it was like, to have no one.

'Please don't do this,' she begged softly.

His hard profile could have been cut from paper with sharp scissors. The line of his brow swept strongly to his aristocratic nose, the mouth, beautifully shaped, had been drawn into a grim line. The sharply angled jaw was clenched. The long black lashes flickered in scorn—or was it relief?

'Andiamo!' He went below.

With a harshly indrawn breath, Alfonso let the boat surge across the canal. He nudged it skilfully into the jetty, and tied up. Guido and the Contessa were ready with their unsuspecting smiles. Guido had a beautiful camel coat slung over his shoulders, and was wearing a dark, pin-striped suit. Flavia shivered slightly in an elegant green wool dress with matching shoes and an emerald green cape flung stylishly around her, so that her emerald earrings and necklace were discreetly visible.

Money, style, breeding. They thought the American would be impressed. Suzy's eyes became distressed. She felt a deep pity for them both. They didn't deserve what was about to happen.

'Contessa!' she cried unhappily.

Too late. Fiorenzo had emerged from the cabin. She saw the Moroschinis stiffen and clutch each other. Fiorenzo just stood in the well of the boat, his dark laser-stare burning into the speechless Contessa while the sullen Alfonso heaved the four cases out of the boat.

'Well, here I am. The prodigal son,' said Fiorenzo softly, breaking the terrible silence. He stepped unhindered on to the jetty. 'Under a false name, maybe, but nevertheless, I've finally made it. Last time, I remember, you set dogs on me. I bear the scars to this day.'

Two pairs of dark brown eyes swivelled to the prominent labels on the luggage, widened in horror and swivelled back to Fiorenzo again. Suzy remembered with a start the scars on Fiorenzo's thigh. Dogs? she thought, aghast. Did the Contessa fear him that much?

'Verreaux? You? *Madonna!*' breathed Guido.

'Be quiet,' breathed his mother. 'Explain,' she snapped.

'Let's go inside and all will be revealed,' said Fiorenzo imperturbably. 'Or shall we hurl abuse at each other in front of the staff and the neighbours?'

'All this luggage...' Flavia's eyes opened wide at the four suitcases. 'You imagine you're staying? For how long——?'

'Till I die.' His eyes mocked her, a cynical smile on his lips. 'However long that may be, Flavia,' he added softly.

The Contessa's face became suffused with anger. She spun her chair on its axle, her hand gripping Guido's arm so that he was forced to go with her. She swept past the bewildered cook and the maid, who half bobbed to Fiorenzo, imagining he was the banker. Who Must be Impressed.

Suzy followed Fiorenzo. His casual manner couldn't conceal the fact that he was gripped by an electrifying excitement. She could tell that by the way he held his body, and she realised he was becoming easier for her to read. That could be useful.

'Suzy? Stay with him!' ordered Flavia sharply over her shoulder, as Guido pushed her into the lift.

Suzy met Flavia's panic-stricken eyes and her heart went out to the woman. 'Like glue,' she said grimly as the lift doors closed.

He surveyed the lower *portego*, the hall which ran the whole length of the building. During the heady days when Venice had dominated the trade routes, the storerooms on either side of the hall had groaned with bundles of silks, sacks of spices, chests of gold and ivory—perhaps even slaves in the barred rooms at the far end. Now it was just a dark, damp, echoing place, the peeling walls showing signs of those times in the recent past when high tide had brought flooding and slowly dislodged the marble flagstones.

Fiorenzo walked along the hall with a proprietorial air, pushing open each heavy, studded door. Alfonso stiffened beside Suzy, and he put down the cases he had assembled under his brawny arms. Curiously she fol-

lowed Alfonso's agitated glance, and saw that Fiorenzo
was trying to push open a door that had become stuck.

'Alfonso! Non riesco ad aprirlo.'

Alfonso shrugged. *'No ha la chiave.'*

He couldn't open the door; Alfonso denied having a
key. The two men eyed one another, Alfonso defiant,
bristling and wary, Fiorenzo with a speculative look.
Suzy couldn't understand why Fiorenzo was bothered
about a store-room. She waited while Fiorenzo came
back to join her.

'Ever been in there?' he asked her.

'No. It's only junk down here. Though Alfonso said
something about renovations when I last came. Perhaps
the room is being done up for something.'

'Perhaps. The lock is new.'

Suzy frowned. 'So?'

'So something important is kept in there,' he frowned.

'But it's none of your business,' she told him sharply.

He smiled his superior, know-it-all smile and strolled
slowly to the stairs, examining everything—the coffered
ceiling, the flaking plaster, the loose tiles. They climbed
the stone steps, the silence broken only by the rustle of
her skirts and the light tap of his leather shoes.

The first-floor hall served as an entrance to the grand
barrel-vaulted staircase. Here, he stopped again, his hand
on one of the brass lion-heads whose mouths carried the
swagged crimson rope which acted as a handrail.
Fiorenzo's head tipped back to survey the richly painted
ceiling of voluptuous women and fat pink cherubs, his
eyes narrowing at the flaking gold leaf.

Flavia appeared at the top of the stairs, facing him
square on, her expression haughty. Above her hung a
delicate crystal chandelier which threw dark and sinister
shadows on her face. Suzy drew in her breath. She and
Fiorenzo could have been carved from the same mould—
both arrogant, imperious, aristocrats to their fingertips.

He started to climb the stairs, never taking his eyes off Flavia for a second.

To Suzy, watching Fiorenzo's dark and penetrating eyes scowling at Flavia from under his brows, it was as if a conqueror had arrived to accept homage from the vanquished. But Flavia wasn't daunted; her icy glare would have cut lesser men down to size. They were fighting their corners. She wondered who would come out on top.

'You're taking one hell of a risk,' said Flavia coldly when he stood towering over her on the top step.

Fiorenzo lifted a cynical eyebrow. 'By standing at the top of the stairs? Are you contemplating a quick thrust forwards of your wheelchair, so I go tumbling down? Not wise, I warn you, not when I have left documents with my lawyers in the event of my death if it should be suspicious.' His words were each spiked with contempt.

The Contessa lowered her eyes. 'What do you want?' she asked in a low tone.

Fiorenzo lifted his head proudly. 'To stay here. My agent has paid enough for the privilege. It's been my dream to come back here under my own terms.' His smile was genuine this time, lighting his eyes and making them glitter like a moonlit sea. 'I want this palace, Flavia!'

'It belongs to Guido. He's the heir, remember? Your father saw to that,' said the Contessa stubbornly.

'His father?' blurted out Suzy, puzzled. 'I don't understand.'

Fiorenzo turned his head to look at her, his hypnotic gaze burning a path into her brain, his excitement making her alert, alive, as if her subconscious mind enjoyed his success.

'How little you know,' he murmured silkily. He folded his arms and hesitated for a moment, then continued, with a mocking glint of his eyes at Flavia. 'This,' he informed Suzy, 'is the aunt who once called me a psychopath.'

'She wouldn't...' Suzy's mouth clamped shut on her denial that Flavia would say such a thing. Something inside her said that Flavia hated Fiorenzo so much that she'd call him any name under the sun. It was a new slant on the dignified Contessa. Her soft eyes searched Fiorenzo's for clarification.

In a swift movement, his hand reached out to flick back her hair from her shoulders. His fingers slid to the nape of her neck and Guido breathed in sharply. Suzy noticed Flavia give her son a hard, shrewd glance as if Guido's concern irritated her. Suzy's head whirled. Being with the Moroschini was like fighting her way through an impenetrable forest.

Fiorenzo's hand was rubbing rhythmically on her neck. She could move if she wanted to. Incredibly, she didn't, and she knew why. A glorious, shimmering sensation was radiating from his fingers and coursing chaotically through her body. Her breasts beneath the soft fichu began to rise and fall with the rhythm of his caress.

'You need a little instruction,' he murmured huskily. 'We'll start with the family history. Flavia and my father, Prince Moroschini, were twins, she being the elder of the two. If she had been born a male, she would have had the title, the wealth, the land, the factory. And this palace. Wouldn't you, Aunty? Oh, such is fate. But my father inherited instead.' The warmth of his fingers and the pressure became deeper, more difficult to ignore. 'Is there something bothering you, Guido?' he enquired innocently.

Guido's mouth compressed. He said nothing, his eyes fixed on the ground. Suzy quailed at the look Flavia was directing at Fiorenzo, who mercifully released her from the sensual touch of his fingers, leaving his hand possessively on her shoulder.

He's claiming me, she thought, and wondered why.

'But if the palace belonged to your father, why does the Contessa own it now, and why does Guido have the title? Surely if your father was Prince Moroschini, you should have inherited,' she frowned.

'Good lord,' he drawled. 'She's come to the same conclusion that I did!' He moved close to her and tipped up her chin with his fingers and thumb so that he could look straight into her eyes. They blazed with fire—a mixture of electrifying vitality and determination. 'We both made the same mistake, Suzy,' he said with a soft urgency. 'Of course I should have inherited the title. However, Flavia manipulated my father so that Guido could inherit. I had no idea what I was up against. Flavia was ambitious for her son. She has the madness of motherhood on her side.'

Suzy gasped. That was virtually blasphemy in this country.

'Don't speak of my mother like that!' began Guido sullenly.

Fiorenzo abandoned his hold on Suzy and took a threatening step towards his cousin, who retreated behind the wheelchair. Fiorenzo smiled unpleasantly. 'That's right, Guido,' he taunted. 'Hide behind a defenceless woman. Or are we all fooled? Is she stronger than a cart-horse?'

'You have no human feelings whatsoever,' grated the tense Flavia, her eyes showing alarm.

'Will you make it plain to me why you aren't the heir?' asked Suzy doggedly, trying to divert the two men from open battle. She knew who would win.

'My father disinherited me,' he said coldly.

'I gathered that,' she replied drily. 'You haven't said why.'

'Ask her.' Fiorenzo's bitter, contemptuous jerk of his head indicated Flavia, and Suzy's eyes asked the silent question.

'Suzy, dear, imagine this man as an uncontrolled child. My brother was appalled at the monstrous creature he had fathered,' said Flavia in a small, trembling voice. 'First the rages and tempers, then a cold, unresponsive silence. My brother said he'd rather the dustman became the next prince of this House than Fiorenzo——'

'Well, he got close,' commented Fiorenzo, with an arrogant stare at Guido.

'Ohhh!' gasped Flavia.

'You'll pay for that insult!' grated Guido.

'I'm sure I will,' said Fiorenzo coolly. 'The fact is, Suzy, that I have been disinherited, like it or not. It's legal; I checked. I heard from the lawyer, who eventually traced me a month after Father died. I didn't actually *know* my father was dead, but there we are.'

'That's awful!' she said in dismay.

'Isn't it?' His eyes had gone opaque, and Suzy shrank at the impotent fury bottled up inside his tense body. 'But never mind. It's all water under the bridge now.' He gave a short laugh. 'It was almost water over me, too, wasn't it, Flavia? How fortunate I am that Suzy came along.' His voice hardened. 'Now what I want to know is, why did Father deny the custom of centuries and nominate my kinsman for his heir?'

'He hated you!' seethed Flavia.

'No. Sorry, that isn't good enough,' said Fiorenzo mildly. 'Blood is blood. He would *never* have willingly repudiated me. Not with the family motto ingrained in his heart. "Secure the bloodline, pure and true". It seems quite inconceivable to me. So that leaves coercion.' His dark eyes brooded on Flavia, betraying his feelings.

'He needed no coercion, not the way he felt about you!' Flavia muttered.

'True. You whittled away my character for years,' said Fiorenzo flatly.

'You were trouble from the moment you were born!' Flavia countered.

That was unfair, terribly unfair, thought Suzy miserably. She was aware that Fiorenzo's body was quivering with suppressed rage. His eyes became small pinpoints of light in his poker-face, and she wanted to run and comfort him. She grew still. The situation wasn't what she'd thought. Fiorenzo had good cause to feel resentment towards his father. Though not towards Flavia; he was unjustly accusing her of everything from attempted murder to assassination of character. His mind had been twisted. She came out of her thoughts to discover he was speaking.

'. . . You're involved in a massive fraud, Flavia,' he said softly. 'And I intend to find out what, however long it takes me. I won't be denied what is mine. For the moment, the title is legally Guido's. So the arrangement is this: you will give me the palace and I will remain silent about your taxes and your secret indiscretion. It seems a neat solution.'

'People will talk! When they know you've come back, they'll wonder why Guido should give his family home to you. They won't expect such charity from him,' said Flavia triumphantly.

'I've already worked that one out,' smiled Fiorenzo. 'That's why you and Guido must not go away, but must appear to live in harmony with me. One happy family, reunited at last, all differences forgotten,' he finished, with a sardonic lift of his mouth.

Suzy turned to stare at him in amazement. 'What would that achieve?' she asked.

'It would amuse me,' drawled Fiorenzo.

'You cruel, calculating——'

'Suzy!' interrupted the Contessa sharply. 'What if we fight you?' she asked, turning to Fiorenzo.

'I tell the taxman about your evasions, and make sure your creditors know that you're virtually bankrupt. And the whole of Venice will learn about your lover. More to the point, I would tell Guido.'

Guido squared his shoulders. 'I know Mother had a relationship a long time ago. She told me. I've said to her that I have no wish to know about something that happened in her past. It's none of my business,' he said hoarsely, 'and it's certainly none of yours.'

Fiorenzo laughed softly. 'If you only knew——'

'Be silent, Fiorenzo!' screeched Flavia. 'Don't you dare say any more! All right! I agree to your blackmail!' She waved down Guido's protests. 'Guido has the title, you have the palace.'

Suzy was open-mouthed at the extent to which Flavia would protect Guido.

'And she stays,' said Fiorenzo softly, flipping his index finger in Suzy's direction.

'I *can't*!' cried Suzy, aghast at the idea.

The Contessa gave a little moan. Fiorenzo's mocking eyes flicked from Flavia to Suzy. 'Go on. She's expecting you to run to her. She'll turn her tearful eyes on you and make you feel a heel for not falling in with the plans of a cruelly disabled woman, the unhappy victim of fate. Admire her technique, while you succumb.'

'You worm!' muttered Suzy, taking no notice of his arrogant chuckle as she hurried over to the Contessa— who was fighting her tears. Suzy pushed back the twinge of doubt. Of course Flavia would be upset; Fiorenzo had merely predicted that fact.

'I'm sorry. I know how you feel about being under the same roof as him. I know it'll half kill *me*,' mumbled Flavia. 'But what choice do we have? If we don't do as he says, he'll talk. You know the situation. He's blackmailing us, Suzy, and there's nothing we can do. Please stay. I need your support. You're so strong.'

Consternation in her face, Suzy stared down at the Contessa. Then she whirled to face Fiorenzo. 'How you can do this, I don't know! It's so cruel. Why don't you just go the whole hog, and be a real villain—tear off butterfly wings and drown a few puppies while you're at it? It's not only the Contessa and Guido you're ruining. You're going to damage my business if I have to stay here——'

'So I will. You can always try to start it up again one day,' he said casually.

She looked at him in amazement. 'You are *deliberately* smashing my business?' she cried.

'Yes,' he confirmed curtly, a fierce light in his eyes. 'Got it in one. And I want to watch you wriggle. Like Flavia, Guido, Alfonso,' he added with a husky growl of pleasure.

'You are so full of vengeance that you don't know how inhuman your behaviour is!' she said resentfully. 'You can't break up people's lives——'

Her arm was jerked by the Contessa's strong hand, and Suzy felt herself being pulled down.

'Suzy, leave it for now. We'll get him out somehow,' promised Flavia, whispering quietly so that Fiorenzo couldn't hear. 'If he stays, he'll hold this secret over me till I've signed everything I own over to him. Blackmailers are never satisfied. Please, help me to protect Guido! I have one or two plans up my sleeve. Stay for now. Appear to agree. We'll allay his suspicions for a while. Trust me. Have I ever let you down?'

Suzy struggled with her conscience and her sense of self-preservation. Her conscience won. It would be awful if Guido thought Alfonso was his father. She ruthlessly dismissed the thought that Guido had few signs of princely blood. Princes didn't all have to look like...

She frowned, knowing she'd intended to say 'like Fiorenzo' to herself.

'How's the persuasion going?' murmured Fiorenzo.

'I'll stay,' she told him coldly.

'Thought you might,' he said smugly. Suzy flashed a look of annoyance in his direction, and he laughed. 'You'll all be paid well for the entertainment you give me,' he said insultingly. 'You'll still get your rent, Flavia, so, Guido, you'll be able to trot around to Florian's and Il Corte Sconta, and buy bait to go fishing with Alfonso. Suzy, you'll be paid in full by Flavia because she'll be able to afford it, and she'll have fun plotting all kinds of dirty tricks to get rid of me.' He beamed. 'So we're all happy, aren't we? Show me my room, Suzy.'

'I'm not your servant——' she began proudly.

'Show me!' he commanded, challenging her to defy him again.

She bit her lip. They were all in his power. He was enjoying every second of it, judging by the glitter in his dark eyes. She tried to resurrect her old hatred of him. The alternative—of sympathising with his cause—was too dangerous. So she lifted her skirts and stalked over to the upper stairs which led to the bedrooms, and Fiorenzo followed.

'You're a brute!' she said crossly.

'If I am, it's Flavia's fault——'

She jerked her head round and glared at him, her hands on her hips in furious defiance. 'That's typical!' she exclaimed scornfully. 'Everything is everyone else's fault, isn't it? Well, let me tell you,' she grated, warming to her theme, trying to feel incensed, 'people hold their own destiny in their hands. You can overcome a hard background, given the will to do so. You're the product of your own making, so, if you don't like what you are, don't blame the Contessa. She's been very good to me, and I won't have you slandering her. Do you hear?'

'Your loyalty does you credit,' he said in grudging admiration. 'And I'll remember how fiercely you defended your mistress when I'm tempted by your sweet lips and want to taste them. Now show me my room,' he finished softly.

Fiorenzo climbed the stairs slowly, his eyes taking in the paintings of the Moroschini princes and princesses. Slowly he walked up, one threadbare-carpeted step at a time.

And, as he moved, he seemed to have forgotten Suzy, because a change was gradually creeping over his face, and she saw there a naked rawness that clutched at her lungs. She couldn't help it. Whatever reason he'd been loathed by all who had known him, it was an unhappy situation.

'Mother,' he muttered to himself. He stood silently before the painting of a tiny woman, dainty, fragile, sweet-faced. His brooding eyes flickered to the massive canvas beside it, hanging in an elaborate gilt frame topped by the Moroschini eagle.

'Your father?' asked Suzy curiously.

He nodded, appearing to search the figure in the painting as if it would tell him something. He turned away, his jaw clenched tightly, and Suzy made no comment, but led him to the double doors of the master bedroom.

He hesitated, then followed her in. Suzy had come here once or twice to speak to the Contessa. She had always loved the oriental-style room with its embroidered satin walls and red lacquered furniture. There was a wonderful view from the canopy-draped balcony, right down the Grand Canal to the beautiful dome of Santa Maria della Salute which dominated the skyline.

She turned on the lights and the room came to life, glimmering in the soft glow of the chandelier. Quietly she went around lighting the tall candles in the silver candelabra perched on carved and painted candle-stands, the light flickering on her solemn face.

'Mirrors behind the bed!' marvelled Fiorenzo. 'I thought that was a Hollywood invention. These must be sixteenth century.'

At his quietly spoken comment, Suzy's head slowly turned to look at him. His fingers were stroking the Fortuny hangings around the bed, revelling in their soft, silky feel, the candlelight emphasising his princely bone-structure. He glanced up at the high, painted wooden ceiling, its reds and golds now a little faded.

'Wait a minute, haven't you been in this room?' she asked, a little surprised.

His mouth twisted. 'I've hardly been anywhere in the *palazzo*. Certainly not here,' he said slowly, turning around to take in every detail. 'It was my father's room.'

'*What* did you say?' cried Suzy in astonishment. 'You haven't ever been in your parents' room?'

'Never.' His mouth tightened briefly. Then he flung open the full-length windows and let in the cold, sharp air, breathing it in harshly, his face half turned away from her, and the candles guttered in the sudden draught, then became steady once more.

'Fiorenzo,' Suzy said, compassion tugging at her heart. 'I wish you'd tell me your version of this feud. You don't help yourself by being so cryptic.'

'I don't like remembering.' His jaw tightened.

'If I'm to be in the middle of it all, I should at least know the background. I still can't believe that your father hated you and wouldn't see you.'

'He didn't even like being in the same country,' he said in a remote voice, watching a barge carrying paintings for renovation go by. 'I lived in the attic here, he lived in Switzerland. Sometimes I was allowed in the servant's quarters. Slept, lived, ate, played there. For seven years. The rest of the palace was out of bounds.'

Suzy went cold. The same attic-room that she had now. It would have been dark and frightening to a little boy. And he was the prince's heir. It seemed bizarre. 'There must have been a reason why the Contessa banished you,' she said stubbornly. 'Guido indicated that you were a little demon.'

'As a baby?' he countered in a low tone, swivelling around on his heel so that he could see her distressed face. 'A baby can't be naughty, Suzy.' She stared at him mutely, not wanting to believe him. 'I told you before. I was unwanted. I was left to cry alone till I had no more tears.'

'Oh, God!' she breathed, distraught. 'Tell me why, Fiorenzo,' she pleaded.

'Why do you tempt me to reveal myself?' he growled. 'I don't want to open raw wounds. My heart has bled enough over the years. Dammit, woman, don't cry! Why are you looking so upset? I was the one who grew up without love, not you.'

Suzy drew the back of her hand across her eyes. 'Because if it's true, it hurts me,' she said unhappily.

His brows met in a harsh black line. 'You feel pain, for me?' he muttered. 'Don't. Flavia will only disillusion you.'

'But I want to know! Why were you unwanted?' she asked vehemently, determined to know more.

'You know perfectly well that my mother died when I was born.'

'But——'

'Hell! Has Flavia told you to turn the knife? Is that what she was whispering about? God! I would have thought you had too much sense to jump through every hoop she holds up, as Guido does.'

'Fiorenzo,' she said miserably, 'I'm asking not because the Contessa told me to, or because I want to hurt you, but because I want to know why a man shouldn't love his son, why he'd treat him so cruelly. Was he mad, as the rumours suggest? And why were you so difficult to manage——?'

'All right.' Fiorenzo sat on a black lacquered chair and motioned her to sit on its twin near by. 'I might as well tell you. Your common sense might prevail and you could even end up believing me.' He was silent for a long time, and then his black brows drew together and he began to speak in a low, toneless voice. 'My father never got to know me. He refused to see me when I was born. He loved my mother so much that he went into deep shock when she died and couldn't bring himself to look at the child who'd killed her. Can you imagine that? To feel so strongly for someone that your life virtually ends when they die? I hope that never happens to me,' he said harshly.

'I hope it does to me,' Suzy breathed, her eyes on his harrowed face. 'I hope to find someone to love utterly, madly. I want nothing less.'

The darkness of his eyes made her tremble. There was an elemental flash of longing within them that drew her breath to the top of her throat. He had a power so compelling that she felt an immediate turbulence in her body when he wielded it, and she knew he had the ability to love as passionately as she, if only he'd allow himself to, if only he'd trust a woman enough.

'I envy the man you will one day love,' he said quietly. 'Find someone worthy, Suzy. Someone who has the same intensity of passion as you, who won't be overpowered by it, who will match you, kiss for kiss, hunger for hunger, who has the same uninhibited attitude to sex.' His expression became pained. 'Not a man like me,' he said quietly to himself. 'I cannot give, only take. I cannot love.'

'Of course you can!' she cried. 'You have it all locked away—look at the fever that grips you when...' Her voice had grown husky. She cleared her throat, not knowing why she had been so vehement in his defence. 'When you talk about things that matter to you,' she finished lamely, her brain whirling at the way he'd looked at her.

He smiled. 'No. Believe me, I've been involved with enough women to know that I can feel no deep emotion for people. Flavia has soured me to the gentle sex,' he said sardonically.

'I think you've misjudged her. You ought to talk to her about the reason why you were treated as an outcast. Perhaps your father demanded it. She tried to do the decent thing and bring you up, while all you did was make things difficult for her.'

'She had no choice. Father said he was going off to Switzerland, my mother's home where she'd been buried. He told Flavia that, if she wanted a home in the palace after her divorce, she had to take me on.' He shrugged. 'She had her own baby—Guido. She cared nothing for me. *I know that.* I was treated like an interloper in my own father's house. I exploded with temper, yes. Wouldn't you, if you were physically active and were shut up in an attic all day?'

'Y-e-e-s, I would. But... Oh, I don't know what to think!' she cried in exasperation. 'Did your father ever come back to Venice?'

'The first time was when I was four or five,' he said. His face became bleak. 'I remember him coming up the stairs, with Flavia, Guido and me at the top,' he reflected grimly. 'He kissed Flavia, hugged Guido, and walked right past me as if I didn't exist. He didn't want to acknowledge that I was alive. I think I began to plan my revenge then.'

Suzy believed him. No one would invent an appalling rejection like that. 'You were sent away to live in Switzerland. Near your father?'

'No. We had no contact. I was furtively farmed out to a poor relative of my mother's, who needed the money. The woman had a hard job. By then I was incapable of responding to affection. I must have been a swine to bring up.'

'But you came back here to visit sometimes?'

'As a teenager, with my savings from weekend jobs.' Fiorenzo rose, thrust his hands in his pockets, and strode up and down the Oriental rug at the foot of the bed. 'I wanted to see my ancestral home, to forge some links with it. Most times I wasn't allowed in. If I did sneak indoors, I was soon thrown out. Once I arrived when Father was on a visit. He didn't know who the hell I was, though I kept telling him. He never left Venice again. Maybe he *was* mad. I don't know. I'm going to find out. Do you want to help me?'

'Me? How? I—I can't help you...' Suzy's voice died into nothing at the desolation in his face. It seemed reasonable that a son should want to know about his father, and his story had touched her deeply. 'Well, I——'

He caught her arms urgently, and drew her to her feet. 'I have to know!' he said. 'Make enquiries. You have the skill; no one will be suspicious of you. Why would he stay in Venice when his heart was in Switzerland?'

She looked at him in concern. Her instincts were telling her that he had been honest, and that there was something fishy going on. She struggled to make sense of the situation. 'You're suggesting he was a prisoner?' she said, sounding doubtful.

'I don't know. It seems far-fetched,' he admitted. 'Someone must have seen him during those years he stayed like a hermit within these four walls. A builder, a plumber... What about servants? Do you know who Flavia employed? Can you find out?'

'She used contract cleaners. No one else. She only began doing lunches for tourists and letting the palace when your father died.'

'I must know if he was ill or held against his wishes, or mad... Good God! I could go mad too! Help me. I have a right to know.'

'Yes,' Suzy agreed with an outrush of breath, succumbing to the earnestness of his plea. 'You have. I'll ask the Contessa——'

'No! She mustn't find out that you're doing this for me. Don't you see...?' Fiorenzo shook his head in exasperation. 'It's no use. I can't explain everything. I can't trust you. But do this one thing for me. Find out everything you can about him. Will you?'

'And if I do?' she asked cautiously.

His arms dropped away. 'Very cool,' he said expressionlessly. 'You want something in return. Right?'

'Yes. I do. Give up your hostility to Flavia and your obsession with revenge.'

'Never. After all you've heard? You can't ask this of me, Suzy,' he insisted, sounding disappointed and annoyed.

'Fiorenzo, I can understand your bitterness at being denied your inheritance,' she said. 'But you hadn't contacted them here for six years; perhaps your father thought you were dead——'

'It didn't take the lawyer that long to trace me,' said Fiorenzo grimly. 'If Father nominated Guido purely because he thought I was dead, the lawyer would have been legally bound to search for me at the time of the disinheritance, which was before Father died. No. My father must have disinherited me because it was his considered decision. And I suppose that was his right. Yet...I know in my bones that there's something more to this and Flavia is covering up her tracks.'

Suzy sighed. 'I wish you'd all thrash this out between you. It seems to me that you've had a raw deal. I do understand your resentment. But why do you care? You're a rich man, you have money and power and a highly successful life of your own. You have no ties with Venice——'

'No ties?' He stood stock still, shaking his head at her. 'Suzy, this city is in my blood, whether I want it to be or not.' His eyes became distant and his voice soft as he recalled a memory. 'A few days ago, when I arrived, I stepped out of the airport and into another world. The lagoon. The waiting *vaporetti* bobbing up and down on their moorings, and, in the distance, Venice itself. *La Serenissima*. Sitting on the water-bus watching the skyline fill with domes and bell-towers and medieval houses, I felt a surge of pride and excitement that was pure possession. I've lived in many beautiful cities, taken holidays in all the exotic places in the world. But this is my city and it has been in my blood for hundreds of years.'

Suzy's heart seemed to be branded by his passion. It was something she could understand, for she knew the lure of the city. For him, denied it for so many years, with a fierce pride in his ancestors within him, it must be in his every breath. Instinctively she knew that he would never give up his attempt to know why his father had disinherited him. It was a poignant situation. Two cousins, fighting for their rights.

'I know how you feel,' she said huskily. 'But would you try to reverse your father's dying wish? Remember Guido and your aunt cared for him during his declining years. Perhaps he was acknowledging their affection. It's no wonder he thought highly of them. Can't you accept that and be grateful to them?'

'You're priceless, Suzy,' he muttered. 'Do you always think so well of people?'

'Do you always think so ill of them?' she countered sadly.

His mouth twisted. 'Experience has taught me to.'

'I'm so sorry for you,' breathed Suzy, her face unhappy.

'Don't pity me,' he said grimly. 'It gave me a hunger that was savage and powerful enough to build an empire. It gave me the motivation to prove that I needed no one. That I stand alone.'

'How sad.'

'But invincible. I can't be hurt now.'

'Are you sure about that?' she asked slowly, searching his face. He met her eyes for several long seconds, but she learned nothing from them. He'd closed up again. But there had been progress; he'd talked to her, revealed some of himself to her. He might soften yet.

'A word of advice,' he said, ignoring her question. 'Don't let Flavia's condition persuade *your* soft heart to be affected so much that you get involved in anything illegal. I'm watching you all very carefully. One step out of line and I'll crush you with my bare fist. Understand?'

'But your aunt has agreed to let you have the palace——'

'You're very innocent and trusting for an investigator,' remarked Fiorenzo drily. 'Flavia hasn't meekly accepted the situation. She'd rather die first. I'm threatening everything she's worked for this past thirty or so years. Perhaps even before that. She's dedicated her life to Guido.'

'Yes,' said Suzy, remembering how fierce the Contessa had been about her son. And the plans she'd said she had in mind. 'What will she do?' she asked nervously.

'Use your imagination,' he muttered. 'So far, for a clever woman, you've had your eyes shut where Flavia is concerned. She means to kill me.'

Suzy refused to hear what he was saying. 'You've got a persecution complex!' she accused.

'OK. Have it your own way.' Fiorenzo came over and took her hands in his, holding them as a friend might. A flood of compassion went through her, softening the lines of her face. 'Suzy. If I have an accident in the near future, I want you to investigate it.'

'I'm sure you won't,' she said in alarm.

'I'm absolutely convinced that I will. Wouldn't you arrange one, if you were Flavia?'

'No, I wouldn't!' she cried hotly.

He raised her hands and kissed them both, his dark eyes veiled. 'That's the difference between you and Flavia,' he said. 'How would you feel if I were dead, Suzy?'

Her eyes told him. Through her mind raced the thought of this vital, fierce man, suddenly still and lifeless. It was unbearable. 'No,' she whispered, shaking her head at the image she'd conjured up. 'No!'

Fiorenzo's eyes blazed. 'You wouldn't like that? Wouldn't it be easier if I were dead?'

Suzy stared at him mutely. He moved backwards to sit on a huge armchair, pulling her with him and lifting her bodily on to his lap with a rustle of her long skirts. He silenced her cry of protest with a long, warm kiss. Her arms slid up to his shoulders and they intended to push him away, but the kiss was so sweet that they delayed for a wicked while. And that delay was fatal.

CHAPTER SEVEN

FIORENZO'S kiss deepened. His arms enclosed her in a glorious circle of strength and, to her astonishment, Suzy found her own arms were lifting languidly up so that her hands could thread through his glossy dark hair. It was soft and silky to touch, and she let her fingers move over his scalp, knowing that what she was doing was inflaming him further and causing him to breathe more heavily.

'Suzy,' he whispered in her mouth. 'Sweet Suzy.'

She knew she should stop him. Her brain kept telling her. But she'd wanted this, subconsciously, for so long that she coaxed herself. One kiss, or two, or three. There was no harm. Everyone kissed nowadays without a second thought.

The tip of his tongue explored the pout of her lips and flickered at the corners. She moaned. A frightening energy filled her body, urging her to abandon all restraint and release some of her own inhibitions. And she became afraid of what this would lead to.

'Such soft lips,' he murmured.

'Fiorenzo,' she said, sounding harsh. 'That's enough.'

'No, no.' He frowned. 'More. I'm crazed with wanting. God knows how I've kept my hands off you. I want to touch and feel, to kiss, to look. You're very beautiful.'

'Oh, Fiorenzo!' she breathed.

Why should she deny herself something she wanted? Shaking from the intense ardour in his face, Suzy found herself taking his head in her hands and making him kiss her again, hard. And suddenly it seemed that they couldn't get enough of each other's mouths, moaning and fighting for contact, pressing into each other's bodies with an abandon created by a long denial, his hands twisting in her hair to hold her captive.

They drew back a fraction and her fingers reached out to discover the texture of his cheekbones. Satin and iron, she thought with pleasure.

'I want you. I need you,' he whispered hoarsely.

Her eyes closed with ecstasy, and he kissed each lid with a soft, gossamer touch of his lips. 'No. No, Fiorenzo——' It was good. Beautiful. She wanted more.

'Yes. Let me,' he said, his hand thrusting in her long hair. He buried his face in the fragrance of her waves and then began to nibble her earlobe.

'No——' She pushed him away and stared at him with wild, frightened eyes. Kissing was one thing, but... 'No, Fiorenzo, we can't——'

'We have,' he murmured, kissing her neck, inch by inch. He groaned. 'We have and we will.'

His breath sounded ragged. Suzy felt a helpless desire to surrender. But in the back of her mind was a nagging doubt—that Fiorenzo could be wicked, through and through. She shouldn't trust her instincts. She'd been wrong before. Her hand levered beneath his chin and he stopped nuzzling her throat in surprise.

'I want you to let me go,' she said in a flat tone, her body rigid.

He groaned. 'You still believe Flavia?' he marvelled. 'Well, I'll have to find another means of persuading you, won't I?'

'You calculating——! Are you saying that you kissed me to get me on your side?' she raged. He was right. There wasn't an ounce of feeling in him, other than sex and revenge.

He smiled non-committally. 'Whatever the reason, I didn't get very far,' he said ruefully. 'We might learn a little more about each other tonight.'

'Tonight?' she said warily, wishing he'd let her go. It was uncomfortably intimate, sitting on his lap, in his arms, with his smooth golden face an inch or two from hers.

'You will protect me,' he stated with satisfaction. 'You'll be my bodyguard and stick with me, through thick and thin.'

'Why the hell do you think I'll agree to that?' she asked in astonishment.

'Because if you don't, I'll tell Guido who his father is.'

'That's unfair!'

'Life's unfair. Some of us take advantage of that fact.'

'The Contessa said you'd hold that over us, like the sword of Damocles!' she snapped, shaking with anger and frustrated need—which he'd aroused, rot him. 'You bastard!'

'No, no. Guido is the bastard. A fact Flavia is doing her level best to hide. She would take a dim view of your refusing to look after me with Guido's good name at stake.'

'What do I do tonight?' she said sarcastically. 'Sleep on a pallet at the foot of your bed?'

'You could sleep in it, if you like.'

'With you on the pallet.'

'Don't be obtuse, Suzy,' he sighed, the pad of his finger lightly touching her sulky mouth. His other hand slipped to her breast. She shuddered and tipped her head back in an involuntary movement. Fiorenzo slowly undid her laced bodice, and she made a half-hearted attempt to stop him, hating herself for needing his touch, defenceless against the infinite seduction of his smouldering eyes, his ruthless mouth, which even now was savouring the sweetness of her nipple in a gentle, persistent tugging movement that turned any potential refusal into a groan of pleasure.

Warmth flowed through her arms and legs, turning them into liquid weakness. 'No,' she moaned in desperation.

He groaned. 'Dinner,' he said in a muffled voice, lifting his face from her hair, where he had been inhaling its fragrances.

'What?' she mumbled. Suzy vaguely heard the sound of a gong echoing through the palace. She didn't want to move. She didn't want a reason to leave.

'I think you'd better go and change,' he smiled with lazy, contented eyes. Gently he pulled her to a sitting position. 'God!' he breathed, kissing her full lips. 'You're irresistible!'

'I—I must go,' she whispered, her body leaping at his impassioned words.

'Yes. Quick. Before I lose my mind again.' Fiorenzo helped her trembling fingers to adjust her gown. He dropped another kiss on her swollen poppy mouth. 'We have all night.'

'No, I——'

He hustled her to the door. 'See you at dinner,' he said with a wicked, conspiratorial grin.

Suzy staggered to her room on shaking legs which seemed to have a will of their own. She couldn't begin to think, only to shower hastily and dress like an automaton. The dinner gong sounded again and again, with an imperative, angry clanging. She didn't have time to do anything with her hair other than drag a brush through it, or to cover the ravages of her face with make-up. She looked flushed, sparkling, *loved*.

Slipping into the lift, she tried to compose herself. She wasn't even sure whether she was thrilled or appalled, only that she had to shut out what had happened until she had time to sort out her chaotic mind. The lift doors opened and she was face to face with Fiorenzo.

His arm reached around her waist. 'Ill-met by the dining-room door, proud Suzy,' he murmured, kissing her neck.

'Please, Fiorenzo!' she whispered, her eyes alarmed.

His eyes glowed. 'Soon I will have everything I want,' he husked. He pushed her into the dining-room, to face a furious Flavia.

'I would like to make it clear,' said Flavia coldly, 'that being late for dinner is not only rude to me, but it makes the servant's job very difficult.'

'Sorry,' murmured Fiorenzo, pulling out a chair for the dazed Suzy. 'We lost all track of the time. You know how it is.'

He tenderly helped her into the chair. She suddenly became painfully aware of everyone's eyes on her, appraising the state she was in, Flavia's icy eyes noting Suzy's glowing skin, her tumbled hair. She groaned inside, realising her whole body was telling them what had happened.

'Suzy!' breathed Guido, appalled. 'You—he——'

'Sorry, Guido,' murmured Fiorenzo, nibbling at the beautifully made edible pastry bread-basket beside his plate, crafted for the non-existent American banker. 'All's fair...'

Suzy came to her senses. With a rush of deep mortification, she knew why Fiorenzo had tried to seduce her—and had the nerve to pretend that he'd succeeded. It had been nothing but an amusement, calculated to infuriate Flavia and Guido. He was sitting there, smug and mocking, surveying the red-faced Flavia and the miserable Guido as if he'd just pulled off a coup.

'Nothing that you do is fair,' she snapped. How could she avoid him after dinner without jeopardising Guido's peace of mind? Her brain buzzed with ideas. And she selected one.

His puzzled eyes shifted to hers like lightning. 'Regrets already?' he said quietly.

She gritted her teeth and ignored him, giving Flavia an apologetic look and taking a hasty gulp of wine. The Contessa nodded sympathetically, as if she knew the power Fiorenzo had over women and forgave her.

'I remember when you visited here before that you caused havoc with Guido's girlfriends,' commented Flavia coldly. 'To say nothing of the servant girls we had then. I hope you're not going to force your attentions on this child.'

'Suzy is a woman. I can vouch for that,' he drawled. Waves of shame washed over her. Blindly she rose to go, unable to bear the humiliation. 'Stay right where you are,' growled Fiorenzo harshly.

She couldn't move anyway. Her legs wouldn't allow her to, they were shaking so much, and she didn't know whether that was from his disturbing lovemaking, or her fear, or her anger.

'My head aches dreadfully,' she said weakly.

'I'll take you to your room,' said Guido at once.

'You'll do nothing of the kind. Suzy stays here and eats dinner with us,' drawled Fiorenzo. 'Get her a couple of pills.'

Guido signalled to the maid and requested something for Suzy, whose rebellious eyes scowled at the heartless Fiorenzo.

And then she looked away. He was unbearably handsome. He wore a dinner-jacket, his dark hair sleeked back, a gleaming ebony. His shirt was a brilliant white and there was the flash of gold on the cuffs when he lifted his crystal goblet to sip his wine. He looked every inch a prince, she thought wistfully, wishing there wasn't the hostility between the members of this noble, fractured family. Under ordinary circumstances...

She bit her lip and winced. It was bruised and swollen. Remembering its cause, she forgot her intention and glared at Fiorenzo, who lifted his glass to her, his eyes smouldering with naked desire. A silence fell. Around her, the palace seemed to whisper and breathe.

She fixed her eyes on the frieze of the battle of Lepanto, which raged ten feet up, all around the dining-room. Somewhere in it was Fiorenzo's ancestor. Battles, battles! Four hundred years later raged . one which threatened to split the family apart.

The core of her body grew weak with wanting. His foot touched her leg and began to move up and down. She could have moved away, but it was exquisite. Her face became drowsy and languorous, her movements slow.

He had captured her, she thought in desperation, winning the battle for her body by guile, skill... She gritted her teeth. He wasn't the only one with guile and skill. The maid handed her some pills and she gulped them down, then forced herself to pay attention to the conversation. Flavia was making a valiant effort in front of the maid.

'Have some more wine, Fiorenzo,' she said pleasantly.

'Are these our glasses?' Fiorenzo asked, as the maid filled his goblet with wine.

'Er...yes.' The Contessa looked at him warily.

Fiorenzo abandoned his caress of Suzy's shin and leaned back in his chair, turning the goblet in his long fingers. 'Tell me, Flavia,' he said with deceptive casualness. 'How is the factory doing?' Unreasonably, Suzy felt furious that he could switch himself on and off like an electric light. She was still burning on a high voltage.

Flavia moistened her lips. 'Oh, the usual.'

Fiorenzo angled his head and turned his inscrutable eyes on his aunt. 'I heard it was in financial difficulties. That you were managing it badly.'

Flavia shrugged expressively, her eyes blazing messages at him. 'Is it my fault I have no management training? I've done my best——'

'And Guido. What does he do with his time?' asked Fiorenzo smoothly.

There was a tense silence. Suzy knew that he was leading up to something, and could only watch helplessly. She remembered she had a headache and pressed her fingers to her temple, but no one noticed.

'I am a doctor,' said Guido stiffly.

'Seen many patients lately?' murmured Fiorenzo.

'He only looks after me, now,' said Flavia, keeping a tight rein on her temper.

'I can't be expected to take any interest in business. It bores me,' said Guido flatly.

'Then you are no Moroschini,' stated Fiorenzo with slow deliberation. The Contessa stiffened, her warning glance commanding Guido not to respond. 'Talking of glass,' murmured Fiorenzo, 'I think there's some tiny shards of it in my *granceola*,' he said, pushing his spoon around the spider-crab pâté.

Suzy saw Flavia's head jerk to Guido, and she raised a querying eyebrow. He was white with horror, his eyes searching his mother's as if... Suzy put down her spoon, tense and shaking. It couldn't be deliberate, this glass in the food. Fiorenzo was inventing things... She blinked. On his finger were some minute pieces of glistening glass.

Flavia reached across the table and snatched his dish from him, berating the maid, telling her that the cook would have her wages docked for breakages and for being careless. Fiorenzo applauded when she had finished.

'*Brava!*' he said approvingly. 'Terribly convincing, your indignation. Suzy and Guido will never realise that you sprinkled my crab with glass on purpose.'

Suzy's eyes widened. Just in time, she caught herself and made her voice sound convincingly dull. 'Fiorenzo, what are you saying?' she demanded heavily as if the pills were drugging her. Everyone looked at her in slight concern. Including Fiorenzo, she noticed.

'He's being stupid. A silly joke. I think we're ready for the second course,' said Flavia evenly, beckoning to the maid.

Fiorenzo laughed softly. 'You're a remarkable woman, Flavia,' he said, raising his glass to her. 'A Venetian through and through. You fit this unscrupulous, unyielding city perfectly. You and Venice began with tyranny, moving smartly on to become ruthless and secretive. I find it very sad that Venice is no longer powerful. That she became dissolute and evil.' The maid slid a portion of rich goose on to his plate. 'Consider the once great beauty now,' he continued, his eyes boring into Flavia's. 'Old, decayed, crumbling, relying on commoners for sustenance. I speak of Venice, of course.'

'Liar. I know what you're implying and I take exception to your insults. I would ask you not to refer to personal matters in front of servants, even if you are speaking English,' hissed the Contessa furiously. 'Nor may you discuss business or finance at the dinner table. You have no sense of aristocracy, or breeding!'

'And whose fault is that?' he taunted her. 'It sure as hell isn't mine! I was brought up with servants, remember? I've had to learn how to be a gentleman the hard way. *Damn* you, Flavia! The blood of princes runs in my veins!'

'Not for long, if I have anything to do with it!' she seethed.

'Ah.' He smiled thinly. 'Now we have it.'

Suzy knew that he'd been deliberately tormenting the Contessa to make her angry and say things she didn't mean. She stared at the Contessa in horror. Surely... No! Flavia looked far too hurt. How *could* Fiorenzo be so cruel?

Flavia closed her eyes in despair and jerked her wheelchair backwards violently, grinding her teeth. In a furious temper she wheeled herself out of the room. Guido rushed after her. Suzy could hardly contain her anger, and struggled to remember she was supposed to be feeling weak.

'Say it,' murmured Fiorenzo, 'or you'll burst that beautiful blue dress.'

Unsteadily, she banged down her glass. 'All right, Fiorenzo!' she cried huskily. 'You have behaved appallingly!' She passed a quivering hand over her forehead. 'My head!' she mumbled.

'*Basta! Più tardi!*' said Fiorenzo, dismissing the maid imperiously. He leaned forwards on the table, his eyes probing Suzy's. She sighed, hoping her eyes looked glazed and had reached that delicate point between being cross-eyed and just unfocused. 'Hmm. You don't look too good.'

'I want to go to bed,' she muttered.

'Oh, good,' he said calmly.

Unnerved, she decided to push the boat out. 'Those pills...I never was any good at...' Her voice trailed away. She swayed in her seat and let her eyes slowly close. Fiorenzo was instantly at her side, supporting her. She prayed he couldn't see how frantically her heart was beating, and hoped that she'd made the right decision. She was banking on the fact that he liked his women conscious when he made love to them. She could be wrong.

She heard him heave an exasperated sigh. He rang for the long-suffering maid and asked her to call Alfonso.

Content that her strategy had worked, Suzy settled more comfortably into her chair as she heard the maid's footsteps die away. There were several seconds of silence, seconds when her whole body tingled with expectation and the hairs on her neck rose so that she was sure he'd see them standing up like little waiting soldiers.

His mouth kissed the tip of her ear. 'Sleep well, Suzy,' he murmured. 'I'm damned if I will.'

It was Alfonso who carried her to the lift and up to the attic, the maid who helped her to undress and slip into bed. When she was alone, she smiled to herself. Fiorenzo's plan to seduce her hadn't worked. Her face grew thoughtful. She couldn't have a headache every night. It was too classic an excuse! She pulled the sheet up to her chin. The strange, thudding sound was echoing through the house, irritating her because she did know what it was, but couldn't place it at the moment. She must remember to ask Flavia in the morning.

That night she tossed and turned in the cold little attic-bedroom, trying to weigh up the information she had about Fiorenzo and Flavia. Both could be lying. She couldn't make up her mind any more. Fiorenzo's love-making dominated her brain and her body. She wanted him very, very badly and that fact shamed her.

Next morning, still assailed by doubts and restless with an unfulfilled sexual hunger, Suzy occupied her time in the study sorting bills for Fiorenzo into 'urgent' and 'desperate' while he took some builders around the *palazzo* to see about renovations. Fiorenzo didn't believe in letting the grass grow under his feet.

As she sorted the bills, she was also taking the opportunity to search the desk for anything that might throw light on the last few years of his father's life. She didn't like having unsolved mysteries on her mind.

'Suzy?'

She whirled. Guido. Hesitant and awkward, in the doorway. 'Oh, it's you,' she said. 'I thought it was Fiorenzo.'

'Disappointed?' he jerked out.

'No.' She smiled. 'Highly relieved.'

'Oh, God, Suzy!' Guido hurried over and took the surprised Suzy in his arms. 'To think of that bastard's arms around you, kissing you... I wanted to see you last night, but you'd gone. I was afraid... Did he make love to you? Did he?'

Her hands lay on his shoulders, keeping him at a decent distance. 'No, Guido,' she said quietly.

To her astonishment, he slammed her into his body. She smelled the hot sweat of his body, the taste of coffee on his breath as his mouth opened over hers, wet and searching. After Fiorenzo's fierce but skilled kisses, this was revolting. Her body wriggled as she prepared to slip away.

And then she heard Fiorenzo's step, recognising it immediately, since there was no other man in the house in leather-soled shoes. No, more than that, she thought, remaining quiescent in Guido's arms. She knew *how* he walked. Finding that worrying, she sank into Guido's embrace, steeling herself against the unpleasant kiss and the bear-like embrace.

'My God! You're full of energy this morning, Suzy!' drawled Fiorenzo.

Guido briefly lifted his mouth, his eyes triumphant. 'Push off,' he said, bending to kiss her again.

She became aware of warm breath on her neck and her body trembled, sensing Fiorenzo behind her.

'Careful,' he murmured in her ear. 'Or Flavia will put glass in your food, too.'

She was flung aside by Guido, and staggered, in time to see Guido take a swing at Fiorenzo, who effortlessly ducked and pushed his shoulder under Guido's chest so that the astonished man went flying.

Then Fiorenzo straightened, angling his head in an attitude of listening. Suzy heard it too. The strange thud she'd heard the night before.

'Know what that is?' asked Fiorenzo, his eyes glacial when they turned on her.

'If I did I wouldn't tell you,' she bit out.

'I know,' he said smugly. 'Do you? What is it, Guido? Mama kicking servants?'

'Oh! That's terribly cruel!' Suzy cried.

'Go to hell!' yelled Guido, scrambling to his feet. He stormed out, slamming the door.

'I think I've hit a nerve,' murmured Fiorenzo.

'Why do you taunt him like that?' accused Suzy. 'Especially as his mother can't walk.'

'Because if anyone will crack, it'll be him,' he said coldly. 'And I meant what I said—that you must keep it a secret that you allow Guido to kiss you and run his paws all over your body like a dyslexic gorilla. If Flavia gets wind of your relationship, she'll hurt you.' His hands reached out and caught her small waist, encircling it. 'I don't want you hurt, Suzy.' His hands tensed as if to crush her waist, and she drew in her breath. 'No. Flavia mustn't damage your body. Not when I haven't had my turn yet.'

Her hand cracked across his face hard, leaving a white and then a red impression on his cheek. 'I'm going to prove your father was insane,' she said, driven beyond endurance. 'Then we'll all know what to do with you— have you certified and lock you up.'

'Vicious little bitch,' he growled. 'Wait till I get you alone. I'll show you the difference between a floundering fisherman and a dedicated lover. I swear I'll have you crazed with wanting, hungry for my body.'

He whirled on his heel and left. Suzy groaned. She'd suffered Guido's clumsy kisses for nothing. Fiorenzo still meant to seduce her. She leaned against a bookcase, trying to calm herself down. Maybe it would be easier if she worked as an investigator in the clip-joints of down-town Saigon, she thought wryly. Less wearing on the nerves.

She continued to sort bills. Half an hour later she heard an almighty crash. Her heart in her mouth, she flew out into the *salotto* next door, and reeled back when she saw that the chandelier had fallen from the ceiling of the elegant drawing-room and lay smashed to smithereens. And Fiorenzo lay lifeless on the floor surrounded by glass shards.

'Oh, no!' she whispered. 'Fiorenzo, Fiorenzo,' she repeated, over and over again. She was rooted to the spot, her heart deafening her with the pounding in her ears. The accident he'd predicted. This was it.

A darkness blackened the world for a moment and she swayed against the doorway, fighting the faintness and the hollowing sensation of loss. Let him live. Don't let him die! she chanted inside her head.

'Cristo!'

Her enormous eyes left Fiorenzo's prostrate body, and slowly lifted to see Guido, aghast with horror, in the end doorway, his hand over his mouth as if he was going to be sick.

Fiorenzo stirred. He lived! Dear God, her prayers had been answered. An incredible feeling of relief flooded through her, so strong that she shook with the knowledge that she hadn't wanted him hurt. Ruthlessly she forced herself to come to her senses and went to help him up. Guido still hadn't moved. In a daze, she pulled Fiorenzo to his feet, and he rubbed his back where he'd been lying on a thick rope. His eyes met Guido's.

'Not a game any more, is it, Guido?' he asked softly. 'But a matter of life and death. How far will you let her go?'

Suzy closed her eyes, appalled at the implications of what he was saying. Flavia. Everything pointed to Flavia. She heard Guido's strangled cry, heard him leave, racing down the warren of corridors, and she began to shake like a leaf. Fiorenzo's arms came around her, and weakly she laid her head on his shoulder.

'You can't mean that all this was planned,' she whispered.

His hand tipped her chin up. 'It was planned,' he said gently. 'But don't be afraid, my life isn't in danger. I can promise you that. I think you ought to go to your room. You're in a state of shock.'

She was shaking uncontrollably and quite incapable of thinking straight. Fiorenzo shepherded her to the lift and came up with her to the attic-room, holding her as if she were a piece of precious china.

'I didn't think you'd be so upset,' he said quietly.

She let out a harsh sob. 'Neither did I! I thought you were dead!' she wailed, turning and burying her face in his chest and fighting irrational tears. 'God knows *why* I mind, but I do!' she mumbled into his shirt.

His body went rigid. He stroked her hair gently. 'Would it really matter to you, if I lived or died?' he asked. She nodded her head without speaking, not wanting to let him know that she was crying because of him. 'Then I must put your mind at rest,' he said. 'I'm taking one hell of a gamble, but I can't bear to see you upset.' He pulled her to the bed and sat her down beside him, still holding her trembling hands in his. 'You don't want to see me dead?' he asked.

Her lip jutted out sullenly. 'So it would appear,' she said crossly. 'But I'd probably care for a stray dog, too!' she sniffed stubbornly, appalled at her stupidity.

He chuckled gently. 'Obstinate woman,' he said with affection. His hand curved around her face, the fingers brushing away some tears which had somehow managed to squeeze out on to her cheek. 'Now how did they get there?' he marvelled.

'Nothing to do with me,' she muttered. 'Probably the effects of your eye-watering, splash-it-on aftershave.'

Fiorenzo laughed again. 'You're wonderful. You can't throw yourself away on Guido.'

'Well, he's not stupid enough to stand under dodgy chandeliers when they fall,' she said defiantly, slanting her eyes at him to see his reaction.

He took her in his arms, disconcerting her. 'Now where's that quick mind of yours?' he murmured. 'What do you think the rope was doing beneath me?' Her eyes opened wide, like two green forest pools. 'God, Suzy,' he groaned, 'don't do that. I'm trying not to get distracted.'

She dropped her lashes, a quiver of excitement flickering through her veins. Think, Suzy Carlini, she ordered. Her head lifted. 'The rope was attached to the chandelier,' she said breathlessly. 'Someone——'

'Not someone. Me. I clambered up on the ladder and fixed the rope so I could yank the chandelier down. I arranged both of the accidents,' he said. 'The glass in the food and the smashed chandelier. That particular one was pretty ugly. No great loss.'

'*You?*' Suzy asked, her lips parting in open amazement. 'Why should you ruin a perfectly good pâté and then bring a ton of glass down on your head? Are you insane already?'

'I thought I was sneaky and full of guile, personally,' grinned Fiorenzo.

His finger idly stroked the back of her hand. She let it stay there to prove it didn't bother her. A wicked little voice in the back of her head called her a liar, that she was letting him continue because his touch was irresistible, but she ignored it.

'Explain,' she said, a little huskily, 'this obsession of yours with glass.'

'Guido is frightened. If I can frighten him a little bit more, he'll crack, as I said. It seems the only way to do it.'

'That's...' She stopped, mesmerised by the way his hand was trailing over her palm. Light. Sensual. Suggestive. Her teeth clamped together. It was very hot in the room. Fiorenzo was too close. 'It's——'

'Underhand? Suzy, I'm fighting for my future, for my rights. You must understand——'

'I need some air,' she said faintly. She felt dizzy and bewildered.

'The *altana*. There's a way out at the end of the corridor.'

Stunned, she allowed him to curve his arm around her waist and take her weight as they went along the dark little corridor. She'd thought he was dead, and for a moment it had seemed that her world had stopped and life wasn't worth living. And now he was telling her he'd arranged the whole thing! She gritted her teeth. She could cheerfully murder him herself if only she could find the energy. Shock had sapped it all.

They climbed out on to the surprisingly large wooden platform, high above the roof-tops, where a soft sun had already melted the thin layer of snow and warmed the boards. Suzy hung on to the balcony, the fresh air reviving her a little as she took great gulps of it and tried to get her thoughts in order.

Down below, a gilded funeral barge went by, resplendent in brass, and with black plumes fluttering above the small black *felze* containing the coffin. In the barge rode a surpliced priest, and behind came a convoy of black gondolas bearing muffled mourners. She became aware that Fiorenzo's hand had slipped from her waist, and when she looked at him she saw his face was bleak.

'Are you thinking of your father?' she asked in a low voice.

'Yes. I wish I'd known him. I think I'll go to San Michele to find his grave. And make my peace with him.'

'I'll try to find out what I can,' she promised, putting her hand on his sleeve impulsively.

'Ask nicely and Guido might tell you,' he said bitterly. He gave her a long, slow look. 'Are you and he lovers?' he asked harshly. She shook her head emphatically. 'Thank God!' he muttered. 'I'm sorry if I frightened you just now,' he said. 'I was intending to arrange the accident for later. But I was angry with you.'

'Angry?'

His arm slid up her back. 'I loathed the way Guido was kissing you. You deserve a better technique.'

'It was less crude than the way you kissed me in my hallway,' she reminded him drily.

He grinned at the memory. 'I had to confirm my suspicions that you'd filched my wallet somehow,' he laughed.

'I *thought* at the time you were frisking me!'

'You should trust your instincts more.' His eyes softened. 'I don't normally caress a woman with so little consideration for her needs,' he said huskily.

She was glad. And realised that she'd known that for some time. The pale February sun glowed more strongly, turning his face into pure beaten gold. And she wanted to kiss him so badly that she had to bite her lips to stop herself.

'I must go back,' she whispered, aghast at her wanton needs.

'Not yet. You were really bothered that I might be dead, weren't you?'

She shrugged, wishing he didn't keep harping on about that. It bothered her that she should have had such an intense feeling of despair. 'I said, a bit.'

'How much of a bit?' he asked. She pushed away his hand, which was caressing her cheek. 'I want to wipe Guido's kisses from your mouth,' he said in an infinitely seductive voice.

Suzy couldn't speak. Her throat had closed up. His smile was soft and dreamy. But his eyes were hot with desire. Wordlessly she put up her hands in defence. He swept them away and slid her down to the ground against the chimney-stack in the sunshine. The warm wood smelled faintly of pine. Slowly, as if relishing every second, Fiorenzo moved his hand up her arm, his eyes watching her reaction.

She shook her head in dumb denial, and he smiled. Her head shook again and her eyes pleaded with him. Small kisses burned a trail along her arm, rivalling the sun's warmth. Spring was coming, she thought wildly.

'Fiorenzo, no,' she grated in a voice quite unlike her own. 'Not just sex.'

'Not just sex,' he promised.

He put his hands under her armpits and lifted her into his body, his lips scattering all her senses. She felt the pressure of his fingers as they lazily undid her top button, and she wanted him so badly that she had to clench her fists to stop herself from surrendering.

Her tongue felt thick and as solid as wood. 'Fiorenzo,' she said languidly, as if she were drunk, 'I won't let you, so it's no use trying. I'll yell for help and...all...the...' Her lips had ceased to function. All she could feel was the dizzying spiral of fluid warmth as his marauding hand slid firmly up her shin, beneath her skirt. She was quite still, not even breathing as his hand explored the firmness of her thigh, stroking it with infuriating thoroughness.

'God, you're beautiful,' he growled throatily, his breath harsh and ragged in her ears.

'I—I don't know you——' she began weakly.

'I'm rectifying that,' he breathed.

He drew her right down to the ground, her body surprisingly obedient. Her huge eyes widened as he hovered above her and then covered her body with his, and she pressed her palms into the floorboards so that she didn't clutch him frantically with relief. She found it impossible to understand why the pressure of his body should bring her so much joy and so much torment all at the same time.

He shifted his weight and her green eyes became as deep as jade, her lashes fluttering in alarm. The hardness of him, the power of his masculinity had fired every inch of her, making every pulse throb for him. Slowly, surely, she knew that her body was arching up to his touch.

'Look at your breasts,' he breathed.

In confusion, Suzy peered down her body to see that somehow, with expert skill, he had undone her dress. And now each full, deep, poppy-tipped breast was thrusting up towards him provocatively, the nipples hardening as she watched. Robbed of speech, she could only turn her limpid eyes on him, pleading to his better nature.

'You think I could refuse you now?' he said softly, his lips drifting down to each quivering ruby tip. She shuddered and let out a moan of pleasure and despair. 'Be patient,' he scolded gently, curling his tongue around each breast in turn. His dark eyes smouldered at her for a moment, and then he was suckling her, tugging rhythmically, the flutter of his lashes and his utter concentration and delight rippling through Suzy in a devastating flame that jerked her body violently.

'Yes, react,' he urged. 'Show me what you feel.'

His hands were gentle. Too gentle. Brutally so, teasing, tormenting her. He held her down, repeating his torture, his legs heavy and trapping hers, his hands crushing her wrists as he held them over her head. All Suzy could do was to watch as he sipped and sucked each hot, engorged nipple, her breath shuddering from her in great groans.

'Fiorenzo!' she whispered.

She could stand it no longer, dragging free, pushing his hands away and drawing his head up, holding his face between her palms, kissing him with all the fierce craving that she felt beating within her. Higher slid her skirts, faster pounded her pulses, and she clutched blindly at him.

'Good? You want?' he asked thickly.

'Oh, please, please!' she found herself saying at last. 'Fiorenzo, more. More! *More!*'

He obeyed. With a tenderness and a gentle passion that rocked her body with a desperate need. Someone tore open his shirt. Not her. Someone was moaning huskily like a wanton. Not her. She could feel every muscle in his back, every bone in his spine, the curve of his small waist, the gentle fullness of his hips.

Someone had undone her belt, slid down her dress. Hasty, frantic fingers struggled with the buckle on his trousers, and with equal urgency wriggled them away. And they were flesh to flesh in the cold air, with only two small triangles of white separating them, writhing on each other's skin, feeling the sensual slide of sensitised flesh, aware of every dip, hollow and swelling.

'Oh, *cara*, *cara*,' he moaned into her hip as he discovered its taste.

She drew him up, kissing him fervently, holding his sun-warmed body as if she never wanted to let go. His hand moved slowly up the outside of her thigh, and then his knee had slid between her legs, parting them with a practised skill.

'No,' she breathed.

He ignored her, his fingers ripping off her briefs, and then, with a deep shudder, he touched her. A spasm of need made her body arch, offering him her provocative breasts. She heard a deep growl in his throat and his lips drew fiercely on each hard, painful nipple as he feasted on her body. Suzy closed her eyes in sheer wanton delight. She didn't want to move, only to lie there and enjoy the light flicker of his hand as it rubbed and turned her body into liquid loving. She was floating in a lyrical river of sensual languor, gazing into his passion-drugged eyes.

His fingers paused.

'No, no,' she moaned. 'Go on, go on!'

'Oh,' he groaned. 'I want you so very badly.'

Fiorenzo kissed her passionately, his tongue deep within her, filling her mouth with sweetness, the taste of him, the promise of his virile male body. The ferocity of his kiss made her afraid and elated, his passion clear in the stark desire on his face, his shaking hands.

His tongue stroked along the fullness of her lower lip. Then thrust again. A rage hit her. She wanted to drive him on, to relieve the unendurable emptiness inside her. He was too slow, his arousal of her too long-drawn out. He must touch her. He must.

'I—want—you,' she jerked out.

She gripped his shoulders and his teeth grazed her collar-bone, tongue, lips, fingers, his fierce need matching hers, driving her insane with desire as every part of her seemed to sing, to quiver and stretch towards him, to hunger.

'Suzy, Suzy, Suzy!' he crooned.

'Ohhh . . .'

He had touched the core of her body, his kisses gentle and coaxing suddenly, and he watched her, his eyes compelling and ardent while his fingers worked with a wicked, unfair expertise, and she knew that she was quite incapable of denying him anything he asked of her.

Pliant, biddable in his arms, starved of loving, Suzy gave herself, opening her body to his. They lay skin to skin, desperately pressing against one another as if to seal a bond. He raised himself slightly above her.

Suzy groaned. Through dazed eyes she saw the power of his magnificent chest, the breadth of his shoulders, the beauty of his body. A shudder ran through her whole length, and his eyes smouldered like embers in a fire.

As he lowered his body, her eyes became intolerably heavy and began to close. She felt only the hot silk of him, hard, deep, satisfying, and filling her with sweet strength. Slowly he moved within her, taking his time, but she knew from the terrible grip on her shoulders that he was as crazed as she. That same sultry, croaking voice whimpered, crying, 'Please, please.'

Her mouth was covered by his, their tongues linking, fighting. And she held him tightly, urging, demanding, begging, her teeth savaging his mouth, anything, anything, to make him move faster to release the pent-up feelings within her.

Long and slow he slid, rhythmic, inciting, his breath hot and harsh on her face. He muttered, but she didn't know what he said, it seemed to be far away. Her senses were spinning, the predatory hunger of a man, a woman, responding to the oldest urge of all.

And then he began. Suzy gasped, her body moving with his, supple and voracious, eager and wanton. Her arms twined around his strong, straining neck. She flicked open her eyes with a tremendous effort, wanting to watch his face. Her heart wrenched at the raw emotion she saw in his black eyes.

An inrush of feeling hit her fluid body, and then almost oblivion, as Fiorenzo drove her to the fast climb where there was nothing but sheer sensation. She groaned, shuddered, he held her on a plateau of intense pleasure, which rippled in wave upon wave through every inch of her, until her body exploded with a ferocity that seemed to shatter her into pieces. And then she lay beneath him, her breasts heaving, and she quivered and moaned to herself in a small, weak little whisper.

A glowing, glorious lassitude spread through her. She felt replete. Totally satisfied. Sated. She smiled, sighed and her body went limp as Fiorenzo's head came down to nuzzle softly at her neck.

CHAPTER EIGHT

THE cold, the hardness of the floor and Fiorenzo's weight began to impinge slowly on Suzy's wakening senses. She wriggled luxuriantly beneath him, and he shifted to lean on one elbow, grinning.

'Little did I imagine,' he smiled, 'when I was a lonely child, sitting up here and watching the life-blood of Venice flow past, that one day I'd be making love to an abandoned woman with the body of a goddess and eyes as green as the lagoon.'

An abandoned woman. Was that how he saw her? Suzy felt colder, the sweat on her body chilling rapidly. And she felt cold inside, wondering what her hunger had cost her. She sat up and found her dress. Fiorenzo turned her round by the shoulders so that she faced him, and she shook him off.

'Don't,' she said, trying not to sound shaky. 'I'm cold.'

'And worried. You wonder if you've betrayed Flavia,' he observed quietly. 'Perhaps yourself.'

He seemed oblivious to the cold. She shivered and pulled on her clothes without looking at him, feeling awkward and unhappy, though her body told her a different story. Suddenly tired, she sat down to do up her dress with fumbling fingers. He took over, kissing her as he did each button, and soon she was kissing him back and wrapping her arms around his icy back.

'I don't know where I am or what I'm doing,' she said honestly. 'I'm so confused. I'm not used to behaving like that.'

'Neither am I. Suzy, take a rest. Tuck up in bed and get warm. Relax today while I lure a few builders with promises of untold wealth.' He helped her up. 'And then tonight I will prove to you that Flavia is deceitful, and you will be forced to trust me. This I promise.'

He kissed her sweetly and dressed, leaving her in her room. Suzy let her mind drift for a while, holding the image of his gentle, tender face in her head when he stood in her doorway and smiled at her. How he was going to prove the Contessa's guilt, she didn't know, only that part of her longed for him to be vindicated and part of her couldn't bear the thought of Flavia being a liar.

She couldn't rest. Her body seemed to slowly catch on fire, as if Fiorenzo's lovemaking had invigorated her. She waited until she heard Guido and his mother go out for lunch, with Guido taking Flavia to their favourite bar by the little Fenice theatre.

Then, eager to continue her search for the truth and perhaps to prove to herself that she hadn't allowed a liar to make love to her, Suzy dressed and went downstairs. Fiorenzo didn't see her. He was sharing a plasterer's sandwiches, and had produced a bottle of wine; they were sitting on top of a plank placed across two exploratory ladders, dangling their legs dangerously near priceless silk drapes and discussing the merits of Titian and Tintoretto. She smiled, hearing them, amused that they should have such a proprietorial attitude to two painters who'd died more than four hundred years ago.

After having a snack lunch herself in the kitchen, she continued her search for anything that might help Fiorenzo to learn about his father's years in the *palazzo*. It was as if the late prince hadn't existed. On impulse, Suzy pulled on her coat and went out into the late afternoon gloom, speaking to the nearby tradesmen, to neighbours, to people who had delivered goods to the palace and whose names were on the bills she'd sorted.

No one had seen the old prince, no one knew the exact details of the accident. All spoke of Flavia's great devotion to her twin brother.

Disheartened, she returned late, to find Fiorenzo with his shirt-sleeves up, at the top of another dizzyingly precarious ladder and inspecting with a huge torch the carved wood ceiling in the *anti-sala*. Anxiously she waited till he came down to speak to the respectful builder, and he gave Suzy a grin that showed her how much he enjoyed behaving recklessly, in tempting the gods.

'Don't look so worried, Green Eyes,' he laughed, when he had finished his discussions. 'I don't have nerves.'

'I do,' she muttered.

'Oh, you don't know what it does to me, to hear you say that!' he groaned, taking her in his arms.

'Fiorenzo! The builder——!'

'No,' he said firmly. 'If he feels left out, hard luck. You'll have us one at a time. I refuse to share you.' She laughed and gave him a playful punch. 'That's better,' he said. 'If I want to kiss you...like that...and... that...then I will, wherever we are. Let's have something to eat. You can tell me what you've been doing and I can tell you what I've been doing. Like married couples do. Hmm?'

She smiled wryly. Fiorenzo was hardly the marrying type. He took her to a tiny *campo* beyond the *Accademia* art gallery, near a gondola repair-yard. They peered through the open grid of the wooden gate and looked into the yard. Dozens of glossy boats arced upside-down like black beetles with shiny wing cases, their upholstery safely stored in sheds, the striped oars peeping from a tarpaulin. Sparks flew in all directions into the night as a craftsman worked on the metal blade which every gondola carried proudly on its bows, the six forward

prongs representing the districts of Venice, the lone prong
on the rear representing the Jewish quarter.

Suzy watched Fiorenzo's animated face as he chatted
to the man lovingly repairing a holed gondola, and wondered if he still felt isolated, or if he was more content
now. The men packed up work, and Fiorenzo reluctantly moved on.

They ate in a small family-run *trattoria*—one of the
places he'd visited when she'd been following him. She
smiled, thinking how long ago that seemed. There was
only a choice of two things on the menu, but the food
was hot and wholesome. While they ate their pasta, he
told her of the plans he had for the palace, and she
became quiet, realising how very wealthy he must be if
he intended to carry out all of them.

'And you?' he asked smilingly, as their apple and
cherry strudel was placed before them. 'Did you sleep
all day? Does that mean we can stay awake all night?'

Suzy went pink. She hadn't thought about the night.
She'd been living from minute to minute, wary of the
future. 'I've been trying to track down information about
your father,' she said hastily. 'But I've drawn a complete blank. Fiorenzo, it's as if he was never there. No
one's seen him, people have only heard about him, telling
me how the Contessa spoke cheerfully about his health,
but they could see she was tired and upset. I think I'll
have to ask Guido.'

'No.' He frowned. 'I don't want that. I'll have to have
an accident and force Guido's hand.'

'Please don't.' Suzy gazed at him in consternation. 'I
hate you doing that. It seems to be sly and mean.'

'Reserve judgement,' he said quietly, 'till you have seen
what's going on. Then you'll know how determined
Flavia is, and that desperate measures are needed. She's
not going to give in easily, let alone gracefully.'

When they walked back, he cuddled Suzy into his big coat, and she loved it. The more popular streets were full of Carnival revellers, all in costume, and they took a long time to get back to the *palazzo*, getting caught up in the whirl and swirl of the crowds, and being pushed helplessly in the wrong direction.

She loved it; loved being held closely by him as if he cherished her, loved the noise, the excitement, the happiness of everyone. They both felt a little light-headed, and Fiorenzo hauled Suzy against him and kissed her passionately.

'Oh, Suzy,' he cried in elation, 'I've never felt so free!' He smiled down at her. 'And you've released me. I've found someone I——' He stopped, looking guarded, and, instead of speaking the words he intended, he hugged her hard as if they were parting for ever.

When he drew away, Suzy found her eyes moist. Her heart seemed to turn somersaults. His face was so beautiful, so tender, that she knew for certain that this was the man she loved and would go on loving, whatever happened between them.

'Fiorenzo,' she whispered, quite bewildered, lifting her lips to his.

They were jostled and knocked apart by revellers. For several minutes, Suzy fought the ridiculous sensation of loss at the parting. She had just made a momentous discovery that was so staggering it was all she could do not to yell it out at him. She loved Fiorenzo.

The thought dazzled her. Confused, dismayed, filled with conflicting emotions, she searched frantically for him, desperate not to lose sight of him. Panic made her pulse race with a mounting anxiety, and then, to an almost idiotic joy, she could see his head and shoulders topping the crowd, his eyes intent on her as he fought to get back to her side.

She stood perfectly still, the crowd ebbing and flowing around her and not seeming to touch her at all. Nothing would, it seemed, because she was content, her heart serene.

'Fiorenzo,' she said to herself happily.

The crowd thinned and he reached her, his eyes dancing, and he lifted her in the air, laughing exultantly. 'Let's get back,' he said happily. 'It's almost time.'

'Time for what?' she asked.

'A miracle.'

He wouldn't explain any further. Dreamily, holding her revelation to herself, she showed him a quick route back. Fiorenzo insisted on arriving at the watergate, which meant hiring a gondola at an exorbitant price to cross the canal. Silently they walked along the small jetty and into the cavernous lower hall.

She heard the thudding sound almost immediately. 'What is it?' she whispered, holding his warm, comforting hand.

Fiorenzo smiled enigmatically, dug his hand into his pocket, and selected a key, inserting it in the lock and turning it silently.

Slowly the door swung open to reveal a well-equipped gym.

Suzy's mouth dropped open. Of course. That's why she knew the sound; she'd trained in one for long enough, lifting weights... Her jaw dropped further. On the leg-press lay a sweating Flavia in a tracksuit, concentrating on lifting the heavy weights with her legs in a beautifully co-ordinated rhythm.

Suzy was absolutely stunned. She knew from her own experience how much effort was needed to shift weights like that. Flavia was not disabled. She must have the muscles of a rugby scrum-half.

Flavia was not disabled.

Fiorenzo's face had become hard and cynical. He leaned against the freshly plastered wall negligently, his arms folded, one ankle elegantly crossed over the other. Flavia finished the leg-presses, and slid off the bench lithely, walking over to a tread-mill.

She turned. Froze. Went an ash-white and took a step back to clutch at the exercise bike. 'Fiorenzo!' she rasped.

'Well, you may have lost your disabled classification, but you haven't lost your *memory*,' he drawled, with emphasis on the last word.

Flavia's eyes rounded and her hand flew to her mouth in horror. 'What—what did you say about memory?' she whispered.

'Has the paralysis shifted to your ears?' he enquired mildly. 'Yet another miracle. The lame walk, then deafness strikes.' Then, in a swift change of mood, his expression became vicious. 'You conniving, scheming, cheating——'

'It was only the insurance, Fiorenzo!' she gasped, moving backwards as he advanced on her. 'The accident——'

'Yes. The accident. What happened?' he grated.

'It *was* an accident. I swear, by my son's head I swear!' she cried in terror.

'My God! I have to believe that kind of oath,' he growled cynically. 'So tell me.'

'Your father wanted to see the island villa. He'd pestered us for days, and wouldn't eat till we promised. The villa is half ruined. He fell through some rotten floorboards into the room below and took me with him. He died instantly.'

'So you *were* hurt?' exclaimed Suzy.

Flavia turned pleading eyes on her. 'In dreadful pain! For a while I couldn't move. I—I was thinking of the insurance, even then.' She caught Fiorenzo's jacket-lapel as he stood menacingly in front of her. 'I did it to save the palace,' she sobbed. 'You can understand that, can't you? It was going to fall into ruins like the villa and I couldn't bear that. I thought if I pretended to be disabled we could use the insurance money for restorations. Then we could take in paying guests on a regular basis and, when we had made enough to manage, I'd stage a recovery. You must believe me!' she wailed as Fiorenzo's face remained implacable.

Suzy saw that Flavia was on the edge of hysteria as she battered her fists against Fiorenzo's unmoving body. 'Here.' Suzy put her arms around Flavia. 'I'll come up to your room with you.'

'Still you favour her!' growled Fiorenzo.

'Oh, no!' denied Suzy. 'But look at her! She's had months in that chair! It must have been a ghastly self-inflicted punishment, and it's gone on long enough.'

'God, you're amazing,' remarked Fiorenzo, sounding bewildered. 'Get in the damn chair, Flavia,' he said wearily. 'You look too weak to stand. Suzy will see you get to bed and give you a stiff brandy to help you sleep. We'll have to arrange for your recovery to be a little more rapid than you planned. With me pouring money into the palace as if I'd re-opened the Mint, you don't need the insurance to cough up the cash, nor do you need to perjure yourself into the bargain.'

'My debts——' whined Flavia.

'If I had my way,' growled Fiorenzo, pushing her towards the door, 'I'd let your creditors shove you in prison. But I suppose Suzy will insist that I clear your debts for you. And at the moment I can't refuse her anything. No!' he grated, as Flavia tried to question him. 'Don't ask! Just be grateful someone around here is as soft as butter inside.'

'For a merciless gangster, you're very malleable,' murmured Suzy in his ear. She was rewarded with a cupped hand, rotating over her bottom.

When Flavia had been settled, Suzy quietly shut the bedroom door to find Fiorenzo outside. 'Come on,' he said affectionately.

'I——'

'Do I have to cry crocodile tears to get attention around here?' complained Fiorenzo. 'Listen, Green Eyes. I'm not leaving you alone tonight.' He pushed his hand through his hair and grinned at her flush of embarrassment. 'I mean, I'm not leaving you. I don't think you're safe. Flavia could pull anything, now she knows we're aware that she's been defrauding people right, left and centre. You'll stay with me. Sleep with me.'

'Call a spade a spade. If you want me, then say so. You're using Flavia as an excuse,' Suzy said unhappily.

'No!' He took her gently in his arms. 'I mean, yes. Oh, hell! My darling. I don't want any harm to come to you. You're wonderful, but far too generous. This is the woman who locked her nephew up—a little boy, frightened, bewildered—who ignored him, treated him as if he didn't exist. I'm sorry, but I don't trust her. She has an evil streak. And besides, I love you,' he added softly.

Suzy blinked and her lips parted. Fiorenzo was looking down on her with a grin on his face. 'Would—would you mind repeating that?' she asked faintly.

He frowned in concentration. 'Difficult. Er—It was something like this; I don't want any harm to come——'

She gripped his arm as hard as she could, and he stopped in surprise. 'The *last* bit, you fool!' she cried in exasperation.

'Oh, the bit about loving you?' he asked in mock innocence, gently taking her in his arms. His dark eyes melted into hers. '*Cara*, I don't know when it happened. Perhaps when I glimpsed the tenderness lurking within you. Even though you thought I was a ruthless black-mailer, you had compassion for me.' His hand stroked her hair. 'And I tried not to love you. But every moment I was with you, I became more and more ensnared.'

He kissed her forehead and she leaned her cheek happily against his chest. 'Fiorenzo,' she murmured, 'I'm so happy. I love you very much.' In his embrace, she felt protected and secure.

'I know. It took you a long time to admit that. And now, bed,' he whispered, sweeping her up in his strong arms, carrying her to his room along the corridor, and bolting the door securely. 'Bed,' he murmured, nuzzling into her neck. 'Bed,' he breathed into her ear.

'Bed,' she said dutifully, her heart leaping with happiness.

He made love to her that night in the splendour of the Chinese bedroom, gathering her hungrily into his arms, touching, exploring, adoring. In the mirrors behind the bed she would catch sight of her own body and his, naked, strong, taut-skinned, tangled together in love. It doubled her pleasure to see his back, his thigh, the curve of his neck, her hands stroking him.

He had left one candle burning by the window, and after their lovemaking they were able to lie gazing at one another, drunk with happiness, until they became drowsy and fell asleep.

Suzy was totally at peace. He loved her.

Sometime in the night, however, she woke, choking. Fiorenzo was rolling over and coughing too, dragging on a robe. She was half doped from heavy sleep; it was some time before his urgent voice made sense.

'Get out! Get out!' he was rasping.

'What—what——?'

'Out! The smoke!'

'Oh, my God!' She clung to Fiorenzo, realising that the air was filtering grey, as if a cloud had crept into the room.

'On the floor,' he ordered, pushing her off the bed.

'But—I'm not going without you!' she croaked.

Fiorenzo was beating at the smoking bedding with the broken back of a chair which he'd smashed against the bed-post.

'Get to safety!' he yelled furiously, throwing her a spare wrap.

'Leave you? No! I won't!' Suzy slipped into the robe, dragged down the burning drapes, and began to beat them with a plump cushion.

Fiorenzo pushed her aside and took over. *'Santa Maria!'* he muttered savagely, every word accompanied by a blow. 'I'll kill her!'

Suzy stared at his contorted face. She turned and checked the door, which was still bolted. And then she saw that the floor-length windows on to the balcony were open. 'Flavia!' she cried hoarsely. With a shaking hand she lit one or two candles so that they could see what they were doing. The fire was out.

Fiorenzo straightened, faced her and held out his arms. For a long time they just clung to one another, not wanting to be separated, shocked by what had happened. Then Fiorenzo pushed her gently away and looked deep into her eyes.

'The thought of anything happening to you...' He groaned. 'I love you more than my own life. I never thought I could feel like this about anyone, but...' He passed a perplexed hand over his face, leaving sooty marks. 'You've found something inside me I never knew I had. A caring nature. I'd give up everything, anything for you. I want you to marry me. Without you I'm nothing. With you——'

Suzy started at the hammering on the door. Her head swivelled back to Fiorenzo, her mind in turmoil. He had to know she couldn't bear his children. 'There's something——'

'Wait a minute,' he said gently as the hammering continued and Guido's voice could be heard outside. He detached himself from her clinging arms and unbolted the door.

Guido reeled back at the charred bedding, his face pale. 'She's gone too far!' he breathed. 'She's missing,' he continued flatly. 'I went to see if she was all right, and her bed hasn't been slept in. Her balcony window is open. If she's thrown herself in the canal——'

'No. I don't think she would,' said Fiorenzo quietly. 'But she almost certainly started this fire, probably slipping over her balcony on to ours.'

Guido bit his lip and his eyes pleaded with Suzy. 'She could have killed you,' he mumbled. 'I can't pretend I have any feelings for Fiorenzo, other than jealousy, but you...' His head lifted proudly. 'I must look for my mother. Everything she's planned has failed. What are you going to do?' he asked Fiorenzo.

'You are Moroschini. I will do nothing. Take the villa in Asolo and keep out of my sight,' said Fiorenzo tightly. 'Suzy and I will live here. I can't say I like the idea of your children inheriting the title——'

'They won't,' said Guido curtly. 'Yours will.'

'Fiorenzo!' cried Suzy urgently.

He wasn't listening, but his eyes were glittering as dark as jet as they searched Guido's sullen face. 'Why mine?'

'I acquired the title through deceit,' rasped Guido. 'I return it to you, formally. By rights, it is yours.'

Fiorenzo stiffened. 'Coercion?'

Guido hesitated. 'Not exactly. Your father had Alzheimer's disease.'

'Alzheimer's?' Fiorenzo looked devastated.

'Mother was terrified you'd find out,' muttered Guido. 'He began to lose his memory early on. He even failed to recognise me sometimes. Mother wanted it kept a secret. At first it was pride, then . . .' He shrugged. 'I was able to make his life as comfortable as possible, but he was in a total daze most of the time. That's how mother got him to sign the disinheritance document.'

'And maybe why your father didn't know who you were when you were a teenager,' added Suzy gently.

'I'll leave Venice. I'll wake Alfonso and find Mother.' Guido turned to leave.

'Alfonso drove the police launch that tried to run me down,' said Fiorenzo in a hard voice.

Guido halted, his back still to them. 'Yes. And Mother pushed you in. I didn't know anything about that.' He spun around. 'He did it out of misplaced loyalty! Don't bring charges against him. He'd do anything for Mother, and I have a particular fondness for him. We go fishing together a lot. He talks to me.'

'Yes,' said Fiorenzo tightly. 'He——' Quickly he checked himself. Suzy slipped her hand in his, glad that he had decided to keep silent. Alfonso was almost certainly Guido's father. It was for Flavia or Alfonso to reveal the truth.

'You could have been friends,' commented Suzy sadly. 'Cousins, living together like brothers.'

'And instead we ruined your life, Fiorenzo,' frowned Guido.

Drawing Suzy into the protection of his arms, Fiorenzo smiled tenderly. 'Not entirely. I have Suzy. We love each other. We're going to be married.'

There was an unpleasant laugh from the open doorway. The hairs on Suzy's neck rose as Flavia appeared, looking triumphant. 'Out of the frying-pan into the fire,' she gloated. 'So you love little Suzy.'

Fiorenzo frowned, his dark brows angling like black scimitars. 'I ought to wring your neck!' he snarled, his body tensing.

Flavia didn't seem at all intimidated. 'You love her above everything?' she asked slyly.

Suzy felt faint. Wide-eyed with dismay, she gripped Fiorenzo's arm, her fingers biting into his flesh. Flavia was going to tell him about her barrenness. It was something private. To be told quietly, where she could cry a while and then leave him with regrets. Her mouth opened, but nothing happened because there was a terrible lump blocking her throat. She stared miserably at the jubilant Flavia and for the first time saw what Fiorenzo had meant when he had claimed that she was evil, through and through.

She'd only seen what Flavia had wanted her to see. Always optimistic, she'd never imagined anyone could be all bad. The Contessa knew she was doing wrong. This was cruel, *cruel*!

'What are you getting at, Flavia?' frowned Fiorenzo. 'Of course I love her above everything. Don't think you're going to part us.' He glanced down at the stricken Suzy. 'It's all right, sweetheart, you needn't worry,' he said soothingly. Then he flashed his eyes up in warning to Flavia. 'Hurt her and I will kill you!' he grated. 'She's mine and I'll defend her to the death.'

'I suppose you're planning children, are you?' asked Flavia.

'Oh, my God! Mother——' croaked Guido, realising what was happening. 'You can't do this!'

'It stopped you from considering marriage to her,' snarled Flavia.

'Please——' whispered Suzy, ashes in her mouth.

'What Suzy and I are doing is none of your damn business,' snapped Fiorenzo. 'Only that we love each other. But yes, of course we'll have children. It might annoy you to think that the dynasty is continuing through me instead of Guido, but——' He stopped. Flavia had begun to laugh hysterically. 'For heaven's sake, Guido, what's happening?' he asked irritably.

'Children?' laughed Flavia derisively. 'Goddam you, Fiorenzo, I have the last laugh. You think you have it all! I ought to let you marry her and find out!'

Fiorenzo went very still. 'Find out what?' he asked quietly.

'That you will be the last of the Moroschini! She can't have children! She's tried! She can't carry them full-term.' Flavia's voice dropped to a low, husky growl. 'Now who has everything, Fiorenzo Veronese, the last *Il Principe de Corradino Moroschini*?'

Suzy's numb fingers fell from Fiorenzo's arm. He had frozen like a block of solid ice, was staring blindly with horrified eyes at the empty space where Flavia had been standing. Suzy's eyes squeezed tightly together and, with a sob, she pushed past Guido in blind panic, racing down the stairs and out into the streets, running with no idea where she was going, only that she had to get away.

He hated her for betraying his dreams. Fiorenzo longed for children to continue his dynasty. He adored them. He deserved a dozen. And she was less than a woman and no good to a man who had an aristocratic bloodline to protect. *We love each other.*

'Oh, God!' she cried passionately into the silent street.

She ran over bridges, into blind alleys, across wide squares, not recognising anything. In the end her legs wouldn't carry her, and she sank on to a seat in a *campo* which she dimly recognised as being the Maria Formosa.

We love each other. How hollow those words were now. His love hadn't been deep enough. It couldn't stand the test. The look on his face had been one of stunned realisation. Tears ran down Suzy's cheeks. She leaned back in the seat quietly sobbing, watching a boy tease

a girl who was trying to drink from the water-fountain.
The boy had torn off the girl's shoe and she was pretending not to care.

That's what she had to do. Pretend not to care. She
huddled up, morosely watching the boy, too limp with
despair to go over and thump him as he filled the girl's
shoe with water and taunted her with it. The girl made
a sudden lunge and almost caught the boy, but failed.
So she proudly whirled around and stalked off, leaving
the boy looking foolish and clutching the girl's shoe in
his hand.

Suzy heaved a deep sigh and rubbed hard at her eyes.
It would be the hardest thing she'd done in the whole
of her life—to walk away and leave Fiorenzo. But she
loved him so much that she couldn't inflict herself on
him. He had to be free to find another wife.

She hung her head, fiercely trying to stem the fresh
flow of tears. And didn't notice the contrite boy running
after the girl, returning the shoe and begging for
forgiveness.

Her head lifted at the sound of fireworks, and she
realised that Carnival was drawing to an end and she
had been sitting in the square for hours. Wearily she
rose from the seat, stiff and aching. The end of cel-
ebration, of madness, of behaving out of character.
Ironic.

She took the boat back. On the little square opposite
the Palazzo Moroschini, she stood in the middle of the
crowd gathering to see the grand display of fireworks as
dusk fell. The *palazzo* was a blaze of lights, as if they
were celebrating too.

Tears streaming down her cheeks, she stood, fever-
ishly devouring the beautiful building with her eyes, so
that she would never forget an inch of it. Then she imagined Fiorenzo inside, in every room in the house, visu-
alised him striding around, his shirt-sleeves pushed up

vigorously so that he could clamber ladders and investigate everything that needed doing. It would be a happy household, when he met a woman he wanted to marry. Full of laughter and children...

'Suzy.' Fiorenzo. Choked, emotional.

She whirled. 'Forgive me! I can't—I'm sorry—I was going to tell you but every—thing happ—ened so...fast,' she sniffed, trying to compose herself.

'I saw you, looking at the palace,' he said grimly. 'I couldn't believe my eyes. I thought you'd gone forever.'

'Almost,' she said in a small voice.

'How could you do this to me?' he asked in an accusing tone.

'I'm sorry. I was about to tell you,' she whispered.

'No, you little idiot! I mean, how could you run out on me? I nearly went mad. Guido and Alfonso had to prise me off Flavia when I caught up with her in her room. I almost killed her,' he said, his voice shaking with emotion. 'Oh, my darling, do you think I care more about the damn dynasty than I care about you?'

'What? I—I saw your face,' she said huskily, holding her breath. 'You were shocked beyond all belief——'

'Damn right I was! Sweetheart, you are my life, my love, everything I want. I was aghast that Flavia could be so foul to you. Didn't you *hear* me when I said I loved you? Didn't that mean anything to you?' he asked sternly.

Suzy searched his angry face uncomprehendingly. 'But—but——'

'You've hurt me,' he said in a strained voice. 'If you can't have children, then I'm very, very sorry——'

'Please,' she breathed. 'Spare me the courteous goodbye.'

Suddenly she found her shoulders being shaken sharply. 'You're not listening! I've a good mind to dunk you in the canal till your head clears,' Fiorenzo cried in exasperation. Then he sighed gently at her resentful face, and lightly touched her trembling mouth. *'Cara,'* he husked, 'children or not, it makes no difference to what I feel about you. It's you I love, you I want. Get that into your thick head, Green Eyes,' he chuckled affectionately.

Suzy searched his face. 'Me? But what about the Moroschini line—your sons——?'

Fireworks exploded in the sky above them. The masked crowd roared their approval. Suzy and Fiorenzo never knew. He was kissing her wildly, slowly, thoroughly, convincing her of his love. Their embrace was to continue, on and off, as they crossed the Grand Canal to the Palazzo Moroschini, and to the gallery, where he made love to her. And then in the hastily locked *salotto*, on the priceless Oriental rug. The fireworks rained from the sky, crackling and sizzling, dazzling the crowds outside.

'"Sec—secure." What's "Secure" mean, Father?'

Fiorenzo looked up from the floor where he was sprawled, reading the newspaper. His eyes lifted to Suzy's, where she sat a few inches away. 'Keep safe,' he murmured.

She leaned forwards and kissed his beautiful mouth, then turned to look proudly at her handsome son. 'What are you reading, Claudio?' she asked affectionately.

'This.' Claudio slid off the chair in the magnificently refurbished *salotto* and brought a box over to Suzy.

Fiorenzo sat up quickly. 'Where did you get that? I thought I'd hidden it—— Oh, Claudio!' he said ruefully. 'You've spoilt the surprise!'

'Cos'è? What is this?' laughed Suzy.

'I looked inside, Mama, and——' Claudio put his hand quickly over his perfectly shaped mouth. 'Ooops!' he said, his dark eyes huge at his father's furrowed brow.

'Yes. Ooops,' repeated Fiorenzo drily. He took the box and presented it to Suzy. 'For you, my darling,' he said, kissing her tenderly. 'For all the happiness you've given me.'

'You give me too many presents,' she told him softly. 'All I need is you.'

'And me,' said Claudio, hugging her.

'Oh, yes, *caro*,' she agreed enthusiastically, embracing him. Running feet sounded from the far end of the room. A three-year-old girl with flowing brown hair and green eyes flung herself at her mother. 'And you, Isabella,' laughed Suzy, nuzzling her daughter.

'What's in the box?' demanded Claudio.

Suzy smiled at her impatient, passionate first-born. 'Let's see. Help me open it.' Her eyes met Fiorenzo's as their children each undid a clasp.

'You're not looking, Mama,' protested Claudio.

It was a set of three miniatures mounted together, beautifully painted; Claudio, Isabella and Fiorenzo. Along the base was written the Moroschini motto in Latin and English. And there was space for another portrait. She grinned.

'It's gorgeous. Wonderful. But—"Secure the bloodline"!' she chided. 'I'm doing my best!'

'Whose picture is going in the empty space, Papa?' frowned Claudio.

Fiorenzo came to sit beside Suzy, and lifted his children on to his knees. Suzy felt his hand slip along to lie on her stomach, still flat and firm. The child within her stretched and kicked. She met Fiorenzo's delighted eyes again and laughed happily.

'Now that's something your mother and I have to tell you both,' he said contentedly, his hand clasping Suzy's tightly. 'Good news...'

THREE UNFORGETTABLE HEROINES
THREE AWARD-WINNING AUTHORS

Untamed

MAVERICK HEARTS

A unique collection of historical short stories that capture the spirit of America's last frontier.

HEATHER GRAHAM POZZESSERE—over 10 million copies of her books in print worldwide
Lonesome Rider—The story of an Eastern widow and the renegade half-breed who becomes her protector.

PATRICIA POTTER—an author whose books are consistently Waldenbooks bestsellers
Against the Wind—Two people, battered by heartache, prove that love can heal all.

JOAN JOHNSTON—award-winning Western historical author with 17 books to her credit
One Simple Wish—A woman with a past discovers that dreams really do come true.

Join us for an exciting journey West with
UNTAMED
Available in July, wherever Harlequin books are sold.

MAV93

HARLEQUIN PRESENTS®

A Year
DOWN UNDER

In 1993, Harlequin Presents celebrates the land down under. In August let us take you to Auckland and Northland, New Zealand, in THE STONE PRINCESS by Robyn Donald, Harlequin Presents #1577.

They'd parted eight years ago, but Petra still feels something for Caine Fleming. Now the handsome New Zealander wants to reconcile, but Petra isn't convinced of his true feelings for her. She does know that she wants— that she *needs*—any reconciliation to be more than a marriage of convenience. Petra wants Caine body and soul.

Share the adventure—and the romance—of
A Year Down Under!

Available this month in
A Year Down Under

NO RISKS, NO PRIZES
by Emma Darcy
Harlequin Presents #1570
Available wherever Harlequin books are sold.

YDU-JL